Penny Sumner was born in A
Britain as a postgraduate stud
Oxford. She now lives in New
she lectures in contemporary literature and creative
writing at the University of Northumbria. She is the
author of *The End of April* (The Women's Press, 1993)
as well as *Crosswords*, both mysteries featuring feisty
private investigator Victoria Cross, and has short
stories in *Reader, I Murdered Him* (The Women's
Press, 1989) and *Reader, I Murdered Him, Too* (The
Women's Press, 1995).

Also by Penny Sumner from The Women's Press:

The End of April (1993)

PENNY SUMNER

Crosswords

Published in Great Britain by The Women's Press Ltd, 1995
A member of the Namara Group
34 Great Sutton Street, London EC1V 0DX

First published in the United States of America by The Naiad Press,
Inc, 1994

British Library Cataloguing-in-Publication Data
A catalogue record for this book is available from the British
Library

ISBN 0 7043 4448 3

Typeset by Intype
Printed and bound in Great Britain by BPC Paperbacks Ltd,
Aylesbury, Bucks

For Toni P.,
who has an interest in things catholic

Acknowledgments

First of all I am very grateful to Carol Parris, inquiry agent, for her invaluable insights into how investigations work in the real world. James Morton's *Gangland* proved a useful guide to the history of London's underworld. Yet again Pip and Margaret read the manuscript at short notice and offered, as usual, excellent advice.

PART ONE

PART ONE

CHAPTER ONE

If it's vanilla you're after, go buy an ice-cream.
Hardly original but, given the reputation of the
establishment, somewhat unexpected. I peered higher
up the loo's walls; however, the cubicle's expensive
tiles didn't carry any more graffiti so there was no
choice but to turn my attention back down to my
red stilettos. They were too small. Not impossible,
but small enough to make me hope I wouldn't have
to hoof it.

Giving up on my footwear I reconsidered my top
half. Could I? There was also the issue of should I.

However, I told myself that this was not the time, nor place, to indulge in a spasm of political correctness. As for could — well, as a teenager, I'd been an expert. Pulling a wadge of soft, white paper out of the ceramic holder I shoved two handfuls down the scooped front of my black lycra dress. My bra-size expanded by a factor of ten.

Five minutes later the elevator door opened to reveal the second floor of one of London's plushest hotels. I stepped out into a wide, silent corridor with carpet the color, and texture, of an Oxford-college lawn and wallpaper that shimmered like new leaves. What you pay for is what you get, and in order to stay here you had to pay heaps. As a private detective I find myself in places like this not that infrequently; as a paying customer, well, it'll never happen.

Outside room 205 I took a moment to compose myself. Slinging my bag over my left shoulder I bounced my fingers through my fringe and shoulder-length hair, checked that there was still a gold loop and a diamante stud in each earlobe, and bent to straighten the seams of my charcoal tights. Only then did I knock.

A woman with short black hair and strands of pearls over a navy dress answered. "Yes?" she asked. The question was accompanied by a breathtaking smile.

Another time, another place, I would have had no second thoughts about smiling right back. The reason I didn't was because things weren't meant to happen like this. What was meant to happen was that the son, a sleazeball with a weakness for short skirts

4

and high heels, would open the door. That was the whole point of my costume. One of my colleagues had pulled a similar stunt a few months back and she assured me it was a cinch. The sleazeball answers, he hesitates when you say you have to deliver in person, but then you give a great big red-lipsticky smile, shimmy your lycra, and you're in. Hand the envelope over and then out the door again before they realize what's hit them.

So who was this babe? No mention had been made of a wife or secretary. What would I do if she insisted I give the envelope to her? Our target was only in the country for another twenty-four hours and, if this frightened him off, it would be impossible to get anywhere near him again in that time.

"Can I help you?" It was enough to tell me that her English was perfect, with the sort of accent they specialize in at exclusive finishing schools, somewhere on the Continent.

"I'm a courier," I lied, "with a special delivery for . . ." Oh shit. Unable to pronounce the surname I gave the envelope a perfunctory wave.

She managed to speed-read as it flashed past. "My mother. Thank you, I'll take it to her." A heavily-ringed hand was held out and a cloud of perfume floated along with it.

"Your mother?" What was this about a mother? "I'm sorry but I was told to deliver this message to Mr. . . . There's obviously been a mistake." What was going on here?

She shrugged. "This often happens. My father died five years ago and since then my mother has

5

run the family business. May I have the message please?" Her fingers reached out with more determination, prompting me to totter out of range.

Not father and son at all, mother and daughter! I absorbed this piece of information, and determined to persevere. "Sorry, but I have to deliver in person." I tried a small smile, noticed how delicate her own lip-coloring was, and quickly put a nervous edge to my voice. "Because it's a priority message my boss will check when I get back. I could get into serious trouble."

Her arched eyebrows formed the prelude to a frown, but before she could tell me how impossible this would be, an older voice called out, "It is all right Fadia, show our messenger in."

Where the corridor was woodland glade the room Fadia led me into was autumn garden, smoldering gold and rose. The woman seated in the middle of it had Fadia's eyes and mouth, the same ropes of pearls and heavy rings, but the skin over her cheekbones was paper, the hair white: a worn, elegant woman in her early, or maybe late, sixties. She didn't get out of her chair, and she didn't hold out her hand for the envelope either. Instead she looked me up and down.

"Well." Her voice came from a long way away. "So you have something for me?"

"That's right!" So damned chirpy I almost sang it. "This is urgent and I was told to come straight over." The fact that she didn't even glance toward "this" was worrying, although as far as the court was concerned it was probably enough to drop it into her lap. Because she wasn't a British resident there had to be actual body contact.

"Is that true?" Her eyes closed and a breeze rippled through dying leaves. "A legal document I assume?"

She knew. Of course she knew. "Ah, I have no idea what the messages are about..."

Her eyes opened again and as they looked into mine they told me that not only did she know what was in the envelope, she also knew about the shoes, the dress, the makeup. She knew everything. And, knowing everything, she still reached out her hand. "May I have it please?"

This was so unexpected I didn't react at first, then I thrust it at her.

"Thank you." She laid the unopened manilla envelope on the arm of her chair. "So, you have served a writ on me because my creditors are angry that I have not been able to pay all my debts. And I am to lose my business. This is fate. All my life I have recognized the hand of fate and because of that you really did not need to go to so much..." She looked me over again and this time couldn't suppress a faint grimace of distaste. "To so much *trouble* for my sake."

From behind the chair Fadia laid two protective hands on her mother's shoulders and murmured, "Please go now, please leave us alone."

I showed myself out.

I cursed myself down to the foyer where, before I was able to take more than two unsteady steps, a porter gripped me by the elbow and helpfully propelled me forward. I was, ever so discreetly, being booted off the premises. "Please don't come back Miss," he breathed into my ear, "because on the second occasion we always call the police. I'm sure you understand." The doorman awaited, my hemline offered frighteningly little resistance to a blast of icy wind, and before I knew it I was in a black taxi and we were merging into Piccadilly's late-afternoon traffic.

The driver pushed aside the dividing window. "Where to, love?"

Sinking back against the seat I gave him the address of my flat in Hoxton. Splotches of gray sleet began to spatter across the windscreen.

The divider remained open. "Always the same isn't it?" he called over his shoulder.

In the middle of Piccadilly Circus a disconsolate Eros reigned alone. "Too right," I agreed, "January's always dead miserable."

"No, these posh hotels! As soon as they spot you you're out on your backside. Mean buggers, they don't give you working girls a chance. Got to keep your sense of humor though. I guess you see some funny things in your line of work, don't you?"

He wasn't wrong there. "I guess I do."

"I picked up a lady like yourself the other night, and you know what she told me? She told me she'll never again go with a feller who looks like he might have a dodgy ticker. Lost two like that she has, heart attacks. Ever happened to you?"

I assured him I hadn't lost anyone yet. I didn't know it then but in a couple of weeks' time I wouldn't be able to make the same claim. Unlike his other passenger, however, my client's death wouldn't be due to natural causes.

CHAPTER TWO

April was sitting at my kitchen table, eating an apple. "Good grief," she said, "what do you think you ... I mean, why are you dressed like that, Victoria?"

My lover was herself wearing a pair of paint-splattered dungarees, a holed red sweater, and a black scarf tied over her cropped blonde hair. She looked wonderful. She always does.

"What do I think I look like?" Leering at her I maneuvered some escaping loo paper back into position. "Like a really good time."

"Not like my idea of a good time you don't."

I deserved this but didn't have to be happy about it. "Oh no?"

"Definitely not." Taking aim she chucked the apple core square into the swing bin. "My idea of a good time is, let's see, thirty-threeish, and maturing gracefully. Height? Oh, about five-foot-seven and never, ever, wears heels. Brown eyes, olive complexion, and slim. Small, but perky tits . . ."

I launched myself halfway across the table and landed a kiss on her right cheek. "Sometimes I offer discounts, this could be your lucky day."

Before my mouth could find hers, however, she was sliding out of the chair. "We have six large boxes of china to sort through. I won't be able to help you much after this week you know, I'll be too busy going to lectures and packing my own stuff. You seem to forget we're moving in together in just over a month. Besides —" Her nose wrinkled disapprovingly, "that lipstick would taste disgusting."

It didn't; it was cherry-flavored and I rather liked it. "Oh all right," I said gracelessly. "You win."

Twenty minutes later I was scrubbed and fresh-faced and wearing my good jeans underneath an old sweatshirt.

"Hey, will you look at this!" April exclaimed.

I looked. "Oh. That." April was up in the loft and I was balancing below on the top step of the metal ladder, trying to clip an extra light onto the edge of the trapdoor.

"Tor, this stuff is great! A *black* teapot! Can you imagine what you'd pay for this at Camden Market? Wherever did your mother find it?"

In an Oxfam shop, one Saturday morning. I knew

10

it was a Saturday because that's when my mother used to haul me and my brother Tim around the charity shops. When I think of these expeditions now it's not Ma's face but her hands that I see. Competent, wide-palmed with scrupulous nails, they close in on an object, heft it, hold it to the light, then finally turn it over so the price is revealed. On her left wrist is the watch she always wore with the tan leather band on the outside, so the catch couldn't tear her clothes, and on her third finger is the engagement ring with one tiny diamond, a wartime purchase, and a wedding ring thin as a knife. After her death I sent the rings to Tim in Australia, one for each of my twin nieces.

"Well isn't it?" April's voice demanded.

"Isn't it what? You know, I think it would be better if you took the light and hung it over one of those nails up there ..."

The teapot performed a slow circle over my head. "This is Wedgwood. We're talking serious china here. And it looks old, I don't know, Edwardian maybe. Who would have thought the Edwardians would go in for a black teapot? It could be really rare!"

I gave in. "It isn't Edwardian, it's earlier than that, 1890s, and a black tea set was considered indispensable because it contrasted with the hostess's lily-white complexion. A few grains of arsenic a day and you looked dead fashionable, corpse-pallored with beautiful blue veins."

"Oh." She carefully passed it down to me. "I knew about the arsenic, how do you know about the china?"

Because Ma had looked it up in a book. She was

11

always looking things up in books. I escorted the teapot to the kitchen, where I treated it to a hasty squirt of green Fairy and put it to soak in the sink. What, I wondered, would April come across next? The yellow and blue cow-shaped cream jug? Or the green, art nouveau salt cellar? She'd insist we use them in the new house, there was no doubt about that. Sighing, I returned to my post at the top of the ladder.

After a couple of dusty hours in the loft we took turns in the bath, then dined on fish fingers and frozen peas. I'd videoed this week's *Red Dwarf* and it was halfway through when the phone rang.

"Tor, it's Anchee here." Anchee's voice, disembodied, was redolent of misty Welsh hillsides and gullies; it came with a choir of harps and sheep in the background. In fact she had been born in Hong Kong, and although she'd been brought up in Cardiff it was in the immigrant area known locally as Tiger Bay. Her English was flawless, at school she'd studied Welsh to A-level; but her first language was Cantonese. I often suspected that her thought-patterns were Cantonese as well.

"Hello Anchee." Gulping at my Chardonnay I cursed under my breath: getting an out-of-hours call from the agency's secretary-cum-receptionist can be seriously bad news. Like, you can find yourself spending the rest of the evening freezing in a parked car, desperate to find somewhere to pee, not daring to in case you miss whatever it is you're supposed to be watching.

Her voice was amused. "Don't worry, I'm not sending you off to count milk bottles in Maidenhead."

Thank heavens for that. April had put the video on pause and I gave her the thumbs-up.

"So how did this afternoon go?"

Horrid was the only way to describe it. "Horrid," I said. And then, "It wasn't father and son, it was mother and daughter."

"You're kidding!" There was a strangled giggle. "Hey, you didn't turn up in those manky shoes and that dress, did you?"

"I did." But that was all she was getting out of me; I had no intention of divulging that I'd also been evicted for soliciting. I hadn't even shared that with April. I had, however, told April how I'd acted as a tool of Fate, and although she'd sympathized she'd pointed out that creditors have their own sad stories, and that people with unpaid bills should not be staying in luxury hotels. It didn't help, I still felt guilty.

"It went okay though, didn't it?"

"Don't worry, I delivered the papers."

"Good." There was a rustling from her end. "What I'm trying to do is set up two jobs."

"I'm taking statements all tomorrow," I got in quickly.

"Noted, but this is for the day after. Right, here we are. The first job is for Minna Carp."

Minna is a solicitor who uses us regularly. "Doing what?"

"Oh, photos I think . . ."

The "I think" was an immediate giveaway — she was stalling. "Photos you *know*." And then it dawned. "You can't be serious! Not the gents' loos again?"

"The same. Not the same loos," she rushed on,

"but the same scenario. An indecency case, they need photos of the amount of space under the loo doors. The usual."

"Tell me about it." Two months ago I'd found myself lying on the cold, damp floor of a men's public lavatory, taking photos that would prove to a jury that two young police officers could not possibly have seen what they claimed to have seen from that very same position.

"What's the other job?" I steeled my voice so she'd know that number one was definitely out as far as I was concerned.

"Let's see now, here it is, a Ms. Bry Rocke rang."

I fell back against the sofa in relief. This was for me. I'd done a job for Bry Rocke's sister, Louise, immediately before Christmas and after meeting me in Louise's office one day, Bry had said that she might have some work for me too. I didn't particularly fancy traipsing down to Brighton again so soon, but the agency was surviving on a skeleton crew. My boss, Alicia, was skiing in Tignes, and Stephanie was working on a case in Caracas. Which left either me or Diane to do the photos.

"No problems Anchee," I heard myself say, "Brighton it is."

CHAPTER THREE

Brighton in the month after Christmas was an out-of-season seaside resort trying to pretend it wasn't. In the pre-Christmas period the fairy lights in the shop windows had reflected the cheerful reds and greens of the bulbs lining the Palace Pier, taped carols had rung across the pedestrian malls and the smell of roast chestnuts had wafted from street corners. In the days leading up to Christmas, The Lanes, that maze of narrow, cobbled streets fronted by specialty and designer outlets, had been a crush of shoppers, struggling with bulging bags. But it was now public knowledge that the bags had been full of cheap gifts, destined to pad out lean Christmas stockings. The sale signs now decorating the shopfronts were unashamedly desperate.

This morning's train from King's Cross to the south coast had taken just over an hour and at ten o'clock I was sitting in a cafe in Meeting House Lane, warming my hands around a mug of hot chocolate and watching the determined faces of passersby.

"Sharks."

Had I heard her right? The woman sitting across from me had been staring fixedly at the same scene. Now she shivered, pulled a yellow shawl around her shoulders, and stood up.

"Sharks, the lot of them. We're going to the wall and can't they just smell the blood." I watched as she crossed the street and disappeared into a boutique with *Closing Down* plastered over its windows. The recession was biting hard, although according to an article in today's *Guardian* some areas of the economy were thriving. Bailiffs, for example, were apparently doing quite nicely in the 1990s. So too, I thought, were private investigators; that is if they weren't too picky. At the agency we were still picky, but not to the extent we once had been. Times, however, were tough and when there's a mortgage in the balance a woman's gotta do what a woman's gotta do. With that in mind I hoisted my shoulder bag and stepped out onto Brighton's mean streets.

* * * * *

"So what do you think?" The way it was put this could have applied to either her empty nightclub, which we'd just walked through, or to her long legs, which she herself was currently studying with some approval. I was tempted to approve myself, even though it was obvious that Ms. Rocke was flirting on automatic pilot: if I hadn't been there she would have wriggled her toes just as nicely for the limp aspidistra huddled in the corner.

"It looks like a big place, it must be a lot of work." Her houseplants might be in need of some attention but the green filing cabinet looked new, the taupe carpet was in good nick and the antique furniture appeared to be the genuine article. Sitting on a desk by itself was an Apple Mac computer. Clubland seemed to be paying okay.

Giving a good-humored laugh she reached behind her. "Drink?" That wasn't an herbal teabag she was dangling, but a bottle of bourbon.

"Uh no, no thanks."

"Don't worry, I wasn't expecting you to say yes. I'm glad you could come because Louise says you give good value, and I trust my sister's judgment on something like that."

The fact that she yawned at me wasn't too disconcerting: this was, after all, the end of her working day. She was sitting in a pool of watery sunlight and as she poured herself a glass I gave her a critical once-over, placing her in the late forties. She was an attractive woman, despite the fact that she was wearing too much makeup and the skin around her gray eyes was stretched unnaturally tight. There'd been a time when I'd disapproved of

17

cosmetic surgery, but that was before I'd made a surreptitious visit to a clinic myself. "Go for it," I'd said, my eyes watering shamelessly as a twenty-year-old with perfect skin ruthlessly zapped the broken veins on both my nostrils with an electric needle. Stuff aging gracefully; I wasn't going down without a fight.

Bry Rocke obviously agreed, although right at the moment her carefully-dyed hair was in need of a trim, and when she raised her left arm to replace the bottle I could see that the seam of her red-sequined dress had been allowed to unravel. A woman, I thought, with things on her mind.

"So." It was about time I found out what those things were. "You're having problems with someone fiddling the till?"

Although her glass came up in a mock salute she shook her head. "Actually, no. It's true that I was being ripped off a year or so ago, but I handled that one myself."

If she wasn't having insider theft problems, why had she spun me that line? I breathed deep, settled into the chair and waited. My job involves a lot of waiting.

"You must be wondering why I lied."

I've given up wondering why people lie, I mean the reasons are countless and usually only of interest to them. "Yes, I am," I lied politely in turn.

"Bullshit you are. Why should you a give monkey's? Why, indeed, should any of us?" Her gaze wandered around the room and then came back to my face. "Is Tor short for Victoria?"

Jesus, she was all over the place, but I wasn't

18

sure whether that was the result of the bourbon or tiredness or something else.

"My full name's Victoria." I waited for the inevitable, which didn't happen.

Her eyes half-closed. "The reason I lied, Tor, is that this is a personal matter and I didn't, I don't, want anyone to know about it. That includes my sister."

"Anything you tell me is in confidence." Saying this always makes me feel like a gynecologist, or dentist: open up, I'm a professional. "I will be seeing Louise after this, however, so shall I stick to the petty theft story?"

"Please, I think it's best that way."

"And the real story?"

Her voice was ironic. "The real story is theft, but not petty. Somebody took something, quite a long time ago, and I've only recently discovered how valuable it was. Or rather is."

Uh-huh. Bry Rocke was paying for my every minute so if she wanted to play it slow, slow it was. "How long ago?" I asked. Slowly.

"Twenty-five years."

What's a decade here or there when you've been robbed? Maybe I should have had that drink after all. "You're right, twenty-five years is quite a while. Did you inform the police? Were there any leads on who stole it?" And, by the way, what's the "it" that we're talking about?

She sat forward. "Oh don't worry, I know who took it — the vase that is. It was Perry, the manager of my London club." She looked at me. I looked back. Sighing she said, "I didn't go to the police at the time because, to tell the truth, I wasn't much

19

bothered. The vase had been left to me by a great-aunt, but I'd never really liked it and as it was one of a pair I still had one left. But a couple of months ago I had the remaining vase valued and was stunned when I heard how much it was worth. The valuer then told me that it would be worth up to ten times more if it was with its partner. So, you see, I think that it's about time Perry gave it back."

One vase, two. There were some problems here that I could spot straight off. "He will have sold it," I said.

"Oh no." Sitting back she crossed her legs and I couldn't help but admire her bronzed tights. Or maybe they were stockings? I glanced up to where she was watching me with a small smile. *Touché, Bry Rocke*, that's one to you. She gave a short laugh. "Perry wouldn't have sold it. You must understand that he took it because he really wanted it. And you don't," she added, more for herself than for me, "sell something you want that much."

Not a thief but a genuine art-lover. Who knows? She could be right. "It might have got dropped since then," I pointed out. "Anything could have happened." How much was this vase worth anyway? I mean, did she have any idea of what it could cost, hiring me to trace someone who hit her for a piece of porcelain over twenty years ago?

Her laugh was triumphant, like she was one step ahead. Sensing that in some way she was, I kept my eyes firmly on her face. "It's unlikely to have broken. It's metal. Chinese metalwork, very intricate, very rare, and very old. The vase I've still got has been valued at fifteen thousand pounds by itself." She raised an eyebrow.

I raised two. "We're talking one hundred and fifty thousand for the pair?"

"Yes, Tor, we most certainly are."

After quizzing her for a while longer I summed things up as I saw them. "If we go ahead, you must be aware that after this long it might be extremely time-consuming, or even impossible, to trace him. And, even if I do find him, there's still the problem of how to persuade him to return the vase. I can attempt to negotiate for you, if you want, but I can't force him to give it back." It's surprising the number of people who are disappointed to discover you don't use strong-arm tactics. They expect the office to be decorated with awards for karate and kick-boxing: heaven knows what they make of my B.A. certificate and archivist's diploma.

Her shrug was philosophical. "I come from a family of gamblers and this seems worth the risk. I'm busy until the middle of next week but then I'll do like you suggest, search for some photos of Perry, write down a list of possible contacts. Maybe you could start a week or so after that?"

It would certainly beat sitting around in the office. I followed her back down the long hallway and across the empty dance floor. As I pulled on my heavy black coat and gloves she unlocked an exit into the back alley. "Give Louise my love," she said. "And don't let on about the vase. What happened was my own fault. I should have been a lot more careful."

* * * * *

There was something about Louise Rocke that
always made me think of the tropics, wide verandas
and the clink of ice in dry martinis. Today her
ash-blonde hair was pulled back off her face and she
was wearing a cream silk shirt over olive-green
trousers. Where Bry verged on tarty, Louise was
merely elegant. I preferred Bry.

"You know Tor . . ." She'd insisted on reviewing
my invoice for the work I'd done and was now
taking a checkbook out of her desk drawer. "I still
can't get over it. There I was, dining, so I thought,
à deux, and there you were, hiding behind one of
the damned potted palms."

Behind a pink, marbled pillar actually, but what
the heck. Louise had called on my services after
she'd opened a new business and received
threatening letters, followed by a spate of broken
windows and a botched arson. She'd suspected a
rival company, and had been so sure of herself that
she'd omitted to tell me about the affair she was
having with a rather handsome young waiter. With
my investigation into other office suppliers getting
nowhere I turned my attention to Louise herself and
had followed her dinner companion back, first to
Louise's, and then to his own home. The next
morning I'd sat in my car a few doors along the
road and watched as a woman with a pale, pinched
face shepherded two young children out the front
door.

A couple of hours later I was back in my guise
as market researcher, authorized to pay ten pounds
if she'd fill out a questionnaire on hair-care products.

22

This approach might sound crazy but in its favor is the simple fact that it's nearly always successful. I did my training as a questioned document analyst at Scotland Yard, but what courses like this can never tell you is how to acquire your samples of hand-writing in the first place. If the questionnaire scam doesn't work you can find yourself rooting through black garbage bags in the desperate hope of coming across a soggy shopping list. The drawbacks to this approach are fairly obvious. On top of which, stealing refuse is illegal.

The writing on the questionnaire matched the anonymous letters and Louise had had the grace to be embarrassed. Handing the check to me now, she shook her head. "I never knew recreational bonking could cause such a palaver. If only I'd been honest with you right from the start I would have saved you work, and me money." She tried, briefly, to look contrite. "But really, John's *wife*! I never gave the wife a thought."

Obviously not. "Are you pressing charges?" I hoped not because although I hadn't liked the woman she did have a couple of kids. All she'd been trying to do was survive; the problem was in the way she'd gone about it.

"Good heavens no." Louise studied a set of perfect nails, complete with half-moons. "Oh no Tor, that's not my style at all." She looked up, "As I told you, if you go anywhere near the police word gets out and it has an effect on business. The buying public does not support losers, or victims. Besides, I hardly want the details of my sex life advertised to all and sundry."

She escorted me downstairs. "So you're here to

help Bry discover which member of staff it is that's raiding the till?"

I nodded. "You obviously gave me a good reference."

She smiled. "I most certainly did. I hope we meet again Tor, and do take care."

The door opened as we got to it and a man walked in. He was the waiter, John. Louise put her head on one side. "My new trainee manager," she explained. "A decorative addition, don't you think?"

This way she had John, and revenge on his wife. Louise Rocke might have her own style all right, but it wasn't one that I particularly admired.

CHAPTER FOUR

"Beam me up, Scotty!" At eight the next morning I was in danger of being teleported aboard the Enterprise, with only myself to blame. I'd waxed lyrical on *Star Trek* once too often, with the result that the gang at work had clubbed together and bought me this crazy alarm clock for Christmas. "Aye, aye, Captain." I groped for the off button, tweaked it viciously, and went back to sleep.

A little after eleven I was exiting from the Farringdon Tube, a five-minute walk from the agency which is situated in a side street halfway between the Barbican and Charterhouse Square. We're in a late Victorian building with a firm of accountants on the floor above and a travel agency below. Below that, as Anchee enjoys informing the clients, there's a burial ground containing the bodies of fifty thousand victims of the Black Death. Archaeologists claim this as a conservative estimate.

"Good morning!" None of the mail on the front desk was for me.

"Don't you mean afternoon?" Anchee was in the tiny back room that doubles as kitchenette and junk closet. She was wearing black trousers, a black sweater and silver hoop earrings; I knew this even though I couldn't see her because in winter Anchee always wears black trousers, a black sweater and silver hoops in her ears. Well, almost always; sometimes she wears white, which she maintains is exactly the same as wearing black because if you're Chinese white is the color of death and mourning. When it comes to things Chinese I can never tell if Anchee's bullshitting or not.

There wasn't anything down for me in the appointment book so I helped Anchee out with the invoices. My colleague Diane appeared every so often in quest of coffee or a chat, but most of the time she was glued to her phone in an attempt to trace the whereabouts of a young man who'd made off with a leading art gallery's list of its top one hundred clients. She hadn't commented on how her photo-session in the loos had gone, and so far I'd managed to refrain from asking.

"Can you believe it?" A pair of hazel eyes looked at me from over their third mug of coffee for the morning. At twenty-five years of age Diane was short-haired, with a classic heart-shaped face and a pleasing sprinkle of freckles. Despite virtually mainlining on caffeine she was a serious amateur athlete, jogging most mornings and playing squash and real tennis on the weekends. My exercise consists solely of walking and taking the stairs. And sex, of course. On this I was currently ahead, Diane having entered a period of celibacy after having broken up with Jo, a psychoanalyst she'd been going out with for over twelve months. Diane still insisted her ex had a wonderful mind; I'd found Jo dispiritingly humorless. "Can you believe that even though this guy was only temping, they still let him onto the computer containing all their confidential files! I mean, what do they expect?"

"Have you been able to get a lead on him at all?"

"Not to anywhere where they answer the phone." Looking gloomily out of my window she studied the brick wall opposite. "I was hoping not to have to hit the streets today but there's no avoiding it. It's frigging freezing out there, you know."

I did. My definition of seriously cold is when I have to take my earrings out: this morning my jade studs hadn't made it as far as the agency and were still in my coat pocket. So much for the Greenhouse Effect.

I made do with biscuits for lunch, then put a couple of hours into studying a batch of signatures that had been sent over by Nigel, a forensic scientist I sometimes work for. When I was an archivist I'd specialized in paleography, the study of handwriting. This had led to working on forgeries and questioned documents, and the step from there to becoming a private investigator had been, for me at any rate, a

27

small one. I rang Nigel to let him know my findings confirmed his and he boomed at me what he always booms at me, "Still don't regret leaving your job in the archives, eh?"

I told Nigel what I always tell him, that wild horses wouldn't drag me back to the archives. And that's what I told myself all through the next hour as I struggled with paperwork. I mean, who'd want to be an archivist when they could be a private investigator? Who could resist the challenge, the excitement?

Matters didn't improve when Anchee brought through the job list for the coming week. "Give me a break," I complained. "This is nothing but hack work for solicitors. I mean who'd want to do this for a living?"

"Search me." She reached for the biscuits. "I've got shorthand and more computer certificates than you'd believe." Her predecessor, Andrea, had left the agency for a City bank and now earned twice what I did.

"Thanks a bunch."

"And I know what you're going to say next."

"That's a chocolate digestive you've got there in your mitt, not a fortune cookie."

"You're going to say that it wasn't like this in the good old days."

I looked at the list on the desk in front of me. "Well it wasn't."

"Yeah, yeah, you and Alicia only took on stuff too hot for Scotland Yard to handle. Well times have changed honey, and we've all got to pay the rent."

And the decorator, I thought to myself. During the yuppie Eighties the agency had steadfastly retained a down-at-heel air. New carpets? Alicia owned the business and whenever the subject of new carpets, or new furniture, was mentioned she airily insisted that our look was appropriately *film noir.* "The clients *expect* threadbare carpets," she'd argue. "They don't want to feel that their problems are paying for us to have the walls knocked through with fake arches." Alicia and I had been lovers for five years and her resolution on this was one of the things I'd found so endearing about her. But as times change, people do too: Alicia dumped me, came out and married Paul, and acquired an unexpected interest in interior décor to boot. At the end of last summer I'd returned from a week in Barcelona to find my office color-coordinated, peach shagpile and paintwork to match. "Because this side of the building doesn't get much sun," Alicia explained. "This way it feels warmer."

When I'd grumbled to Diane that the central heating was quite adequate she'd expressed surprise. "But don't you see what Alicia's saying? Peach, Tor, as in peachy. Alicia's trying to indicate how warmly she feels about you."

My ex-lover was telling me she thought I was *peachy?*

Diane's office had been redone in soft grays. What, I asked, was the message there? She didn't hesitate. "Gray's neutral and that, on the whole, is how Alicia feels about me. But of course the most significant statement that Alicia's color-scheme makes is indicated by absence, rather than presence."

When Diane joined the agency, fresh from failing to complete a Ph.D. in psychoanalytic literary theory, I'd found her determination to read each and every situation in terms of absences, gaps, the unspoken and the unspeakable, immensely irritating. Increasingly, however, I found myself coming back for more, in the same way that you worry at a gumboil. "Say it in plain English."

"Your room is peach, mine is gray, Stephanie's is cream, Alicia's is blue, and the reception area is white. What's missing?"

The rest of the rainbow: red, purple, indigo ... "Diane, lay it on me in monosyllables."

"Green," she said, "and red. What are absent are the colors of growth and fertility. You see?"

Alicia had had two miscarriages, both early on in the pregnancies. I nodded, "And her room's blue because ..."

"Because she's sad, Tor. You don't need a background in Freud to read that."

After checking through the list Anchee had left with me I wandered out to return it to her.

"Do you have any strong objections to anything I've put you down for?" she asked.

I shook my head. Because I won't do divorce work I get to do more than my share of interviews. As usual, most of those on the list referred to minor traffic accidents. I couldn't suppress a faint sigh.

"Don't despair, there's an old Chinese proverb which says that, like a human being, the calendar is slowest in its infancy. January's always like this; things will buck up next month."

Before January was over I was to come close to being killed not once, but twice. If those old Chinese proverbs were anything to go by it was going to turn out to be one hell of a year.

*   *   *   *   *

Since the beginning of our relationship April and I had spent most of our weekends in Oxford. Now, however, she'd finished her degree and was enrolled at a London college for the one-year legal practice course required in order to become a solicitor. As a result we were now London-based and my Friday afternoons no longer included a mad dash to Paddington to catch the six o'clock Intercity. These days all I had to do was climb into Lucy, my blue G-reg Cortina, and tootle south down Farringdon Road and High Holburn to Shaftesbury Avenue. At Piccadilly Circus I followed Piccadilly along the northern border of Green Park, down along Knightsbridge and Sloane Street, then over Chelsea Bridge to cross the Thames at Battersea Park. How fast I tootled depended on whether or not I beat the rush hour. If my timing was right, and my luck was in, I could make it to April's in half an hour. If my timing was out, and my luck with it, it could take an hour and a half, longer.

April had been married in her early twenties and retained a share in a rambling flat in Battersea. Her ex-husband, Will, and his new partner, Jen, ran an alternative bookshop downstairs, but now wanted to expand upstairs with a coffee shop and gallery. In other words it was time to move. With April's share from the flat, and a mortgage taken out by her parents, we'd found ourselves a house in Balham.

Balham: Gateway to the South. For the first time in my life I was going to live on the other side of the river. The plan was that as soon as I'd sold my flat I'd buy out her parents' mortgage.

Will and Jen, plus daughter May, had moved a couple of weeks ago. Gareth, April and Will's son, was coming to Balham with us. I dumped my shoulder bag next to a pile of law books in the bedroom and as I approached the kitchen heard Gareth's voice edging towards a wail.

"But I'm almost ten years old!" April's reply was lost amid the sound of something boiling on the cooker.

"So it's not fair, treating me like a little kid! Please Mum, please!"

April was sitting at the table, Gareth standing opposite. His hair was brown and slightly wavy, like Will's, but he had his mother's eyes and pale skin, her straight nose and fine jaw. Neither April nor Gareth looked directly at me, although the former did attempt a wave. Sighting a single lemon in the fruitbowl I busied myself making two gin-and-tonics.

"Mum!" When Gareth got like this he was incapable of letting things drop, which was exhausting for everyone concerned. I immersed one ice cube in my glass, and three in April's. "Cheers."

Her smile was wan. "Trail bikes," she explained. "Gareth wants to go trail bike riding and I've said he'll have to wait until he's older."

Until he's older was code for never ever, not in a million billion years. So far Gareth didn't seem to have twigged to this. Tonight, however, I sensed that things were changing: he was almost ten, almost double figures.

"That's what you always say!" he came back. And then, "Dad says I can go."

The kid must be desperate, usually he was very truthful. Out of the corner of my eye I could see his lips whiten and found myself hoping April would let the lie slide. She did.

"I think," she said quietly, "that we ought to discuss this after dinner. You go and tidy your room and I'll give a yell when the soup's ready."

Gareth took the opportunity to stomp out with some dignity and I sank into the chair he'd been leaning on. "Wow," I offered.

"You said it. Trail bikes! What are the other parents thinking of?"

"Maybe they've got half a dozen and it doesn't matter if Thomas minor breaks his neck." April's neck was pale against the dark blue of her sweater and on the left side I could see a faint pulse.

"Maybe. But it's not just because he's my only one, Victoria."

"I know that, I'm not suggesting you're over-protective. It would be crazy to let him go."

"Honest?" In this light her blue eyes were darker than her sweater, as blue-black as a winter sea.

"Honest. By the way, I love you."

"I love you too." Coming up behind me she criss-crossed my breasts with her arms and bent to kiss the top of my head. "I'm glad you arrived when you did, Gareth's always better behaved when you're around."

Later in the evening I gave April a scarf I'd bought in one of the antique clothes shops I'd passed on my way back to the Brighton station. April's thirtieth birthday wasn't that far off and I still had no idea of what to get her. Maybe we could go away for a weekend. Paris even, or Rome. I'd see what cheap deals the bucket shops were offering.

"It's lovely!" She sat cross-legged on the futon

and held the scarf up to the light, revealing a pattern of colored jungle and exotic birds. As she experimented with the scarf I leaned back against a pillow and realized that I was going to miss this flat. The Balham house dated from the 1920s and had undergone bouts of modernization since, whereas the rooms here were constructed a hundred years earlier, and had more generous proportions. The green and white tiles around the wide fireplace were original, there were sash windows and a magnificent ceiling.

"How old do you think it is?" April had rolled onto the floor and walked over to the mirror.

"In the shop they said late Forties, but my guess is early Fifties." I collect old clothes, a hang over, I readily acknowledge, from my mother's charity-shop days. But where Ma was in search of sensible cardigans I'm a sucker for anything with beadwork or a zigzag hemline.

"Did you find anything for yourself?"

"Actually I got a Sixties *knitted*, two-piece suit."

"You didn't!" She made a face in the glass.

"In electric blue. The top has a really nice neckline and great buttons, and I can roll the skirt to whatever length I fancy. I bought a pair of tights this afternoon that should match it perfectly. The suit was a real steal at only ten pounds." I added this last bit in case my Visa card got mentioned somewhere along the line. Where April had never had a debt on her credit card that had lasted longer than a month, mine tended to linger for years. With a joint mortgage on the horizon this had recently become an issue.

"So how was Brighton? Is the older sister also

being harassed by a vengeful spouse?" Turning around she pointed at her head. "What do you think?"

I thought, as I always do, that she looked beautiful. I was less sure about the turban effect but nodded anyway. "Great, but will it stay up like that?"

She pulled out a dressing table drawer, "Hairpins, that's what I need. Go on, tell me about the sister."

I thought back to the meeting with Bry Rocke. "To be honest, when I was down there before and she said she might get in contact I thought she was bullshitting, you know, 'my sister isn't the only one who requires the services of a private detective.' I didn't really expect her to come up with anything."

"How about this?" I looked up in time to see the scarf collapse around her ears. April, however, was undaunted. "I'm listening."

"Well it seems that twenty-odd years ago her club manager robbed her."

"And she's only just noticed?"

"Oh no, she knew she'd been robbed but she didn't know how valuable the item was, so she didn't bother to pursue the matter."

"Uh-huh." Bending forward she wrapped the scarf round her head like a towel. "By the way, what is it that got nicked?"

"An antique, metalwork vase from China. One of a pair. Louise has had the remaining one valued and been told it's worth fifteen thousand pounds."

"Whew!" she whistled through a mouthful of hair pins. "So she wants her other vase returned, and pronto."

"The two together could net a hundred and fifty grand."

"For two vases? Good God!" She spat the pins into her hand. "We must go through the rest of your mother's boxes, there could be a fortune up in your loft!"

"Okay." I sat up.

"You mean it? You won't complain about how dusty it is, or how boring? You'll let me go through all the boxes properly?"

"Yes I will, if you'll do something for me." I stretched out and switched off the overhead light, so the room was illuminated by only the small side lamp. "I'll agree to let you go through as many musty old boxes you want if you'll take off all your clothes and wear nothing but that scarf."

"All my clothes?" she asked wide-eyed. But her hands were already moving to the studs on her jeans.

"Every stitch," I said slowly. "I want to see you with everything off. And then I want to watch what you can do with that scarf."

Which is exactly what I did.

CHAPTER FIVE

"Good morning, Ms. Cross." Bry Rocke's voice over the phone managed to suggest that its mistress was not only wearing eyeshades but also crêpe-de-chine.

"Ms. Rocke." I crossed my fingers. It was Wednesday and after two days of solicitors' interviews I wanted out of my peach-toned office, and soon.

A slight groan at the other end seemed to indicate she was in the process of sitting up. "You

know it's just hit me, how Biblical we are together."
The lady was camping it up for all it was worth.

I laughed, "How so?"

" '...upon this rock I will build my church; and
the gates of hell shall not prevail against it.'
Matthew 16, if I remember rightly."

"You must have attended more Sunday School
classes than I."

Her laughter had an edge. "You better believe it.
In fact I did a nice line in religious ecstasy, once
upon a time. Now about tomorrow, would you mind
very much meeting at the club around eight? P.m.
that is. Mornings, as you might have noticed, are
not my time of day. In fact I'm usually in bed till
noon."

The low growl was familiar, I used to do my
homework to *Pearl*. "And look where that got Ms.
Joplin; we working girls hit the streets by nine.
Seriously, however, I can make tomorrow night but I
hadn't expected you to surface again before the end
of the week, at the earliest."

There was a short silence. "Well no, neither had
I but life sometimes moves quicker than we do
doesn't it? I've found a couple of photos of Perry,
and my old address book with his number and the
numbers of some other people who might be able to
help."

I assumed she had tried ringing and that he
wasn't still in residence. "Good. Eight it is."

"I discussed hourly rates with your front woman,
Anchee, before she put me through, so that's all
settled. Tell them at the door that I'm expecting you.
Oh, and dress is smart casual. No shorts unless
they're slashed silk and you're willing to reveal all."

A slight inflection at the end almost turned it a question. I decided it was probably safest not to answer.

On my first visit the nightclub's environs hadn't looked particularly propitious, but back alleys on a cold winter's morn rarely do. Tonight, however, I was going in via the front door, and from here the perspective was very different. Marble steps, polished brass handrails; *B-Rocke's* only appeared in discreet black lettering when you made it to the top step, the implication being that you had to be in the know to realize the venue existed in the first place. My guess was that the clientele considered itself professional but streetwise.

An enormous, dinner-suited bouncer was stationed inside the portico and, despite the fact that this was a Thursday night, and damned chilly, a healthy number of patrons were either flashing membership cards, or purchasing membership for the evening, in order to squeeze past him. When it came to my turn I explained that his boss was expecting me and his balding head inclined in the direction of a door marked *Staff Only.* "Second right," he grunted.

It turned out to be the third, if you counted the broom closet. Bry was busy in front of the Apple Mac.

"Tor!" Swiveling in her chair she gave me a faint smile. "Grab a seat. I'll only be a second."

Studying her from behind I could see that my client had found time to make it to her hairdresser. The confident way the black silk dress was hugging her suggested there was no danger of any of its seams unraveling. Exclaiming under her breath she punched a couple of keys then switched the machine off. Her plum-colored mouth was rueful. "This early in my working day I'm on coffee, but maybe you'd like a drink?"

"If we're going to discuss your case I'd best stick to caffeine too, or tea if you've got it."

She nodded and picked up a phone. "Coffee for me please and—" She raised an eyebrow, "English Breakfast? Earl Grey? I'm not entirely sure what we've got in the kitchen because I never drink the stuff."

"Earl Grey, with milk."

"You heard that? Thanks. Right Tor," she said, pulling out a drawer, "let's get down to business."

There were two black and white photos of Perry Alms, a pleasant-looking man with wide cheekbones, a strong chin and nose and a Sixties hairstyle that tipped his collar.

"Quite a smart dresser," I observed. Those wide-lapeled suits looked expensive.

"That's right; classy, never flashy. My partner, Charlie Heatton, liked the image he presented, he thought it went down well with the customers."

Something in the way this was said suggested Charlie was on the flashy side himself. "How tall was Perry?" I asked.

"Oh, a bit taller than me, and I'm five-foot-nine. Five-ten I'd say. Possibly five-eleven. Brown eyes and brown hair."

"Do you know his date of birth?"

"He was twenty-six when he left B-Rocke's, so he'd be fifty-one now. His birthday is the thirtieth of

November — Sagittarius. I remember that because mine's on the twenty-ninth and we once shared a party."

"So you knew him fairly well?"

"Yes and no. Charlie had employed him for about two years in his first London club. And then Charlie and I set up B-Rocke's in Mayfair and Perry managed that. As soon as the club was on its feet Charlie and I came down here to start this, which was originally called B-Rocke's Two."

Where, I wondered, was Charlie now? "So Charlie knew him better than you did?"

"He did. And trusted him completely."

"Until he made off with an *objet d'art*."

Her eyes flickered for a second but I couldn't tell what the emotion was. "Yes, an *objet d'art*. An item of great value. He suddenly handed in his notice and was gone. And so was the vase."

"You kept it in the club?"

"I did, we had an office there, much like this, and I had various bits and pieces in it. I kept one vase in the office and the other at home. As I said, I didn't know what they were worth then, otherwise they would have been in a safe. Under lock and key. Which is where the remaining one is now, of course."

In its corner the aspidistra was looking glossier than it had the first time round. I stared at it and shook my head; things didn't feel right, the pieces didn't fit. "How can you even be sure Perry took the vase? Someone else might have swiped it and it could have been a coincidence that he left at the same time. Or someone could have taken it then, so it would look as if Perry had stolen it."

"I know he took it because he told Charlie."

"He told his employer he was a thief?"

She stood up and walked over to the desk. "He phoned in and announced he wouldn't be turning up for work again. He didn't offer any explanation, but he did say he'd taken my vase as a keepsake. This was all so unlike Perry that at first Charlie thought it was a joke, he quite expected him to turn up for work that night. But he didn't, and we never heard from him again. Look." She picked up another photo from her desk and presented it with a flourish. "Here's a picture of the remaining vase."

"So this is it." I wasn't hiding my disappointment terribly well but I'd been expecting something a bit more impressive.

Bry laughed. "Remember, I said I never really liked it. The value, so I'm told, lies in the way the metal was worked rather than in the aesthetic effect. Perry was the only person I can remember who ever admired it."

The vase sat on a wooden table against a lime-green wall. Studying the photo, I said, "Surely that suggests he knew it was valuable? And if he knew that he probably also knew where he could sell it."

"No. You'll have to trust my instincts on this, Tor. It might sound crazy but even though he stole the vase I know Perry was essentially honest. He wouldn't have sold it, I'm sure of that. People can do stupid, even cruel, things and still be good, don't you think?"

Whose goodness, I wondered, was being mooted here? Reaching into my bag I took out a pen and one of the blue notebooks that I start for each new case. "Bry, I want you to try and remember what the word was about Perry at the time. Where did people think he might have gone? Had he moved to another club? Another city?"

"I didn't hear that he was working anywhere else in London."

"I guess no one contacted you for a reference?"

She smiled. "If they had I would have said he was an excellent manager, but w..h a weakness for oriental bric-a-brac. It was strange because Perry got on very well with the clients, and the staff, but when he left I realized that although we had his phone number I'd never been sure where he lived, and although he was friendly with everyone there were no special friends, or none that I knew about. He was an intensely private person I think, which is unusual in this line of business, and was even more unusual back in the Sixties."

"It was in nineteen sixty-nine that he left, is that right?"

"Yes. It must have been around the end of April, or possibly early May. Charlie was really pissed because London was chockablock with tourists and the club was packed every night. We had huge problems replacing Perry, good managers aren't easy to come by and there was no recession then, new clubs were opening up all over. In fact Perry was so difficult to replace that Charlie had to stay up in London for about three months. I was terribly worried because his heart was already playing up."

A dodgy ticker: that probably explained what had happened to Charlie.

She sighed. "After Charlie died I sold the London B-Rocke's. It became a casino, named after the new owner's fourth wife."

"You weren't tempted to sell here?" I can never

43

quite believe that anyone would choose not to live in London.

"No, I was brought up here and have always loved Brighton. My father had passed away shortly before Charlie and so I stayed on, close to my mother."

Leaning back she started doing things with her legs which I chose to ignore. I demurely crossed my own trousered ankles and went on jotting notes in my book. Bry, however, found another way to change the topic.

"I've been thinking about your name some more."

Inwardly I groaned. I should have played along with her fancy footwork. "Oh yes?"

"It's the name of a village isn't it, Tor Cross? Somewhere in Cornwall. I seem to remember a happy family jaunt there as a child. Were you born there?"

"Nope." I'd been asked this one before, more than once. "Nor conceived. And it's Devon, not Cornwall. Tor is short for Victoria." Wait for it.

"Your father was in the army?"

"That's right."

"A Victoria Cross for outstanding bravery?"

"Uh-huh." Ma's hands cradle the medal as she explains that in order to win this you have to undertake an action in which there's a ninety to one hundred percent risk of death. I'd sent the medal to Tim, along with Ma's rings.

"You haven't asked about mine." One eye closed in an exaggerated wink, "What do you think Bry is short for?"

It's surprising how many people have problems with their names. "Bryony, I guess." I couldn't think of anything else, except for Bryan. Maybe that was it, maybe her parents had wanted a boy. I've always thought that was especially cruel, Davida instead of David, Michaeline instead of the Michael they'd set their hearts on. How can people do things like this to their kids?

"Bryton, that's with a 'y'. So there you have it, Bryton Rocke."

"As in Graham Greene?"

"My mother was his number one fan and *Brighton Rock* was her favorite of his novels. In fact she was so far under the influence that she converted, and remains a Roman Catholic to this day."

"I've never read *Brighton Rock*," I confessed. "Greene's not one of my favorite writers."

Bry pulled a face. "Nor mine, which is a great pity under the circumstances."

I insisted that she go through her old address book page by page, looking for the name of anyone who might have known Perry. All she could offer me were three names, with accompanying phone numbers. The first, simply Ray, was a wild card.

"He was a tall man, about thirty-five, balding. He used to come in alone and he did talk a lot to Perry. That's all I can remember about him, I've no idea what his surname was."

"So why is he in your book?"

She looked blank for a second, then light dawned. "Cars! He sold used cars, expensive ones, up in Islington. Charlie was talking about getting a Jag."

"And did he?"

"No," she laughed. "Charlie never even got around to learning how to drive."

There were two other names, the first for a

45

woman who had checked in the coats, the second for one of the barmen. Both had been in their early twenties. Bry drew asterisks next to the names, then simply ripped the pages out and passed them to me. I'd been given less to go on from other clients, but not often. The only piece of information she could think of that would still be relevant concerning Perry was that he was gay. But no, she'd never heard about any lovers; she didn't know if he'd frequented gay clubs on his nights off.

"I have to warn you," I said, "not to be overly optimistic. I understand that potentially there's a lot of money at stake here, but if I can't come up with any leads on these people then that's it."

"I know," she said slowly, "that you'll do your best. That's all any of us can do, isn't it?"

Why was it that, as I followed her down the hall, I had the uncomfortable feeling she expected something more?

I'd caught a taxi back to Hoxton from King's Cross Station and the driver was regarding the For Sale sign on my flat. It had been up for almost two years now and no longer registered with me.

"You been trying for long?" he asked.

I handed him a ten-pound note. "Oh, a couple of weeks. Are you looking for a flat around here?"

He gave a low snort. "From what I've heard the climate wouldn't suit my complexion. Know what I mean?"

I knew. Hoxton was predominantly white with, so rumor had it, a thriving branch of the National

Front. I'd bought here during the boom, thinking I'd be able to sell when I wanted. I'd thought wrong; the housing market had crashed and I was left with louvre windows, paper-thin walls and a chronic case of negative equity.

Soon, however, I was going to be out of here.

I reminded myself of this in the bathroom mirror the next morning. I had a trustworthy tenant for the flat and within a matter of weeks it would be bye-bye Hoxton. After the ritual check for renegade capillaries I slapped on blusher and lip gloss, brushed my hair, shrugged into a navy suit, circa 1945, and headed for the Tube.

The first thing I did when I got to the agency was ring my genealogist friend, Joyce. "Hi there," I said, "it's Tor."

"Hoozitgaun?" she responded in Glaswegian.

With a missing person's case going back any length of time one of the first things to make sure of is that the person you're looking for hasn't died in the interim. Perry's surname was unusual, which was a help, but I knew that a trawl through the death certificates held in the General Register Office at St. Catherine's House would still take a while, even for a professional like Joyce.

"Have you been to St. Catherine's recently?" she asked. "It's a zoo down there these days Tor, it really is."

Next on the list were the pages from Bry's old address book. London's phone numbers had originally been made up of a mixture of place names and numerals. This had changed in the late Sixties, and each of Bry's pages was a mess of crossings out, with the old, alphabetical prefixes scored through and the new numbers written over the top. Perry Alms' number had originally had an SLO prefix, so presumably he'd lived around Sloane Square. Being a club manager must have paid pretty well back in the Sixties, or maybe the area hadn't been quite so fashionable then. After the new number was a large question mark, which I assumed Bry had written in after Perry left with no forwarding address.

I rang the number, on the off chance, and a child answered.

"You want my mummy?"

Mummy sounded harassed and well-heeled and no, she didn't know anyone by that name. She lived in South Kensington and they'd been given this new number when they moved in three years ago.

What I did then was look up Alms in the current phone book. There was no entry under P but there were two other Alms, with the initials F and R. The first number rang but didn't answer so I wrote it down in my blue notebook, with a reminder to try again later. The second was answered by a tenant who said that Ruby Alms had owned the flat for about six months and was currently working as a nurse in Saudi Arabia; if I wanted to write to Ruby she'd forward the letter for me. I scribbled a note to Ruby, asking if she was related to a Perry Alms, and put it in my out tray.

The number for the bartender, Paul Brown, rang but there was no reply. Checking in the telephone book, however, I hit gold: there was a P. Brown matching the number from Bry's book. In other words Paul Brown was still in residence, at a Kentish Town address. After this stroke of luck, however, I got nowhere with Ray, the car dealer, or

Connie Smith, who'd checked in the coats: both numbers were disconnected. Which meant a visit to the Guildhall Library was called for.

The Guildhall is off Cheapside, just along from St. Paul's Cathedral. After doing St. Paul's, tourists visit the Guildhall for a glimpse of the wooden giants Gog and Magog, the capital's legendary defenders; people like me come to use the library, which includes a collection of old telephone directories. There were four volumes of residential numbers for London in 1969 and I dragged the first off the shelf to find no Alms at all. There weren't any for 1968 either, or for 1970. Either Perry had been ex-directory or the phone had been under someone else's name. I couldn't find a C. Smith to match the number in Bry's book so I photocopied the ten pages of Smiths from the 1969 directory, along with four pages of car dealers from the Yellow Pages for the same year. I had more than enough to keep me going for now.

Two hours later I'd worked through the Smiths and matched Connie Smith's phone number with a T.V. Smith at an address in Shoreditch. There were four T.V.s in the current directory and I'd managed to get answers from two, neither of whom knew a Connie. I'd try the others later on. I'd also begun on the task of ringing the Islington car dealers listed for 1969, but for the moment was letting Diane distract me with her story of how she'd cornered the young man from the art gallery.

"And he says, 'What have I done wrong?' "

"So what did you say?"

"You've committed theft. Taking the list of the gallery's clients was theft, attempting to sell it to other dealers was attempting to sell stolen property. He ran through to the loo and threw up."

"Are they going to prosecute?" I personally thought a ticking-off by Diane would be punishment enough.

"Shit no, they don't want the hassle, or the publicity." She ran both hands through her short hair. "You know what struck me when I finally saw him? How much he looked like the owner of the gallery, he could have been his son."

"Really?" The Oedipus Complex, I made a quick bet with myself.

"Yes, it was uncanny. I think it's pretty obvious that while he was working there he went through a version of the mirror stage, in which he recognized his own separate self, and then also recognized the need to break away from the father figure. Taking the names was about claiming his own identity."

As Diane recounted how she'd explained all of this to her bewildered quarry, presumably after he'd reappeared from the bathroom, I steeled myself for the next bout of telephoning. The line I'd decided to use was one which nearly always had people scrambling to be helpful. I was looking for a man named Ray, I explained, who was once a very — here I hesitated — close friend of my mother's. No, my mother didn't know his surname, they'd met at a party one night and, well, these things do happen. Out of the numbers I'd rung so far only one was still a car yard, and the manager couldn't think of anyone named Ray from the Sixties, unless, that is, I meant old Ray Hewson, who'd had a yard up in Woodside Park? A big man, black as coal, his father had been a sailor from Nigeria, or was it the Gold Coast? I thought Bry would have mentioned it if Ray had been black; no, I said firmly, my Mum's friend had been white. He'd replied that I should know and we'd both given a nervous laugh.

"Of course!" Diane was leaning over the arm of her chair in excitement. "By taking the list of names he was taking away power from the father-figure. The list was on computer printout and for him the printout was itself a representation of the phallus! I don't know why I didn't see that before."

Me neither. Nodding agreement with this latest insight I went back to the womblike safety of my office and spent the rest of Friday afternoon telling lies on the telephone.

CHAPTER SIX

"So that's it?"

"Fraid so." Bending down, I picked up two mugs containing the congealed dregs of last night's hot chocolate. Somewhere under the bed was the hot water bottle I'd jettisoned in the small hours.

"I'm sorry to say this Victoria, but it's a bit disappointing. I'd expected, oh I don't know, something *exciting*." As she sat up against the pillows the duvet slid off her shoulders. I love April's shoulders; I adore the nape of her neck.

I sat down again on the edge of the bed. "Apparently it's all in the technique."

"I see." She peered closer at the photo of Bry's vase.

"Speaking of which . . ." Last night we'd both been tired.

Without looking she held up a hand. "You were on your way to get breakfast. I want to be in that loft as soon as possible, we still have a lot of work to do up there. Besides, you promised."

At what stage was it, I wondered, that our Saturdays had become quite so domestic?

By lunchtime there were three cardboard boxes destined for charity piled against one wall of my tiny kitchen, and an equal number, the contents of which were to be washed and kept, piled opposite.

"A penny for them." April was arranging slices of smoked applewood and cheddar on a plate of digestive biscuits.

"I was just thinking that it seems pointless, washing all this stuff now. Why don't we leave it till we move into the house?" The truth was I'd seen enough of Ma's china for the moment.

"Get real, we'll have enough to do, just unpacking. You've got something else on your mind, haven't you?"

I looked out the kitchen window to the dingy vegetable shop opposite, where the thirteen-year-old skinhead son of the owner was leaning disaffectedly against some empty crates. Every time I walked past he poked out his tongue in a cunnilingus imitation; well that's how I interpreted it at any rate. April maintained there was no sexual content in the gesture and I was simply being paranoid.

The cow cream jug looked accusingly at me from over the top of a box. "What I'm thinking about is this new case. There are some addresses I need to check and it's more likely that people will be home on the weekend." Before we'd started on the loft I'd rung the remaining T.V. Smiths, who couldn't help with Connie. I'd also got a reply from F. Alms, who turned out to be Frank, from Illinois. He was an academic who'd moved to Britain five years ago and didn't have any relatives in this country that he knew about. His wife, however, was interested in genealogy so if I did turn up a whole lot of Alms maybe I could let them know? Paul Brown's number continued to ring unanswered.

April handed me my share of the biscuits, a knife and a jar of mango chutney. "How many addresses?"

"Two, both close. One's in Shoreditch, and the other's in Kentish Town."

Nodding, she picked up the pen and notepad from beside the electric kettle. "Deal. I'll do the washing up if, on your excursions, you stop off at Tavasso's deli and buy, let's see, a quarter of chorizo, sliced. Half a pound of kalamata olives. What do you think about *pain forte* for after? You could go to the wine shop next to Tavasso's and get some Muscat de Beaume to go with it, if you like. We're okay for basmatti rice, aren't we? I thought I'd do a risotto. I'll go across the road later on and see if there's any broccoli in, or mushrooms would do. I'll get salad stuff as well."

This sounded like a dinner party. April thrust the shopping list at me. "I know I nag, my love, but we cannot afford, or at least I cannot afford, to call

54

out for pizzas all the time. Fran and her new woman will no doubt bring something very drinkable, so we don't have to worry about that too much."

Fran, of course. "This is the drop-dead gorgeous auctioneer, right? The one she met through that expensive dating agency?"

"Fran says it's a match made in heaven, this woman is unbelievable."

"That's what she always says, she said that about the wrestler."

"She was not a wrestler, she taught self-defense."

"She broke Fran's finger."

"That was an accident."

"Bullshit, April. The woman was a psychopath." Fran had told me some of the more sordid details, in complete confidence. "Coffee," I said. "We're out of ground coffee. I'll pick up some Lavazza."

I liberated Lucy from the lock-up garage I rented two streets away, and we trundled along the Holloway Road before managing to cut across the traffic and through Camden to the west side of Kentish Town. In the late Sixties Paul Brown's address mightn't have had much panache but today the houses and cars all managed to give the impression that they really deserved a Hampstead postcode.

The mid-terrace house I parked outside was well-cared for in that its slate roof was in good nick and the cream paintwork around the windows and front door was fairly fresh. The box hedge, however, hadn't been trimmed over the summer and the drawn curtains had an air about them suggesting they'd been that way for some time. I wasn't surprised when no one answered. My guess was that the hallway was a mess of uncollected mail and advertising bumf.

I didn't mind going door-to-door, although this wasn't great weather for it. There was no one home on either side but two doors down a woman told me that she hadn't seen Mr. Brown for some time, although since she worked during the day she didn't always keep track of the neighbors. She had heard he was ill. She hesitated here but didn't elaborate. What I needed to do was talk to Mrs. King, an elderly lady who'd lived in the street for years and knew all the comings and goings. Mrs. King was opposite, at number Forty-Two. I said thank you and headed across the road.

Mrs. King wasn't at Forty-Two but Forty-Four, and no way could she be described as friendly. "You know him well, do you?"

I explained that my mother was a friend of the family, who'd lost touch, but she shook her head. "Didn't have any family that I ever saw, but that sort don't, do they?"

What sort did she mean? I tried to look as if I knew what she might be talking about. "Um, Paul was always a bit of a loner, according to Mum."

"Loner!" She sneered, wiping floury hands on a tea towel. "Been better for him if he had been, wouldn't it?"

Mrs. King and I would never get on, that much was obvious. I managed an ingratiating smile. "I really don't know much about him, but it is important to Mum so if I could find out how to get in contact . . . The place looks pretty shut up now."

"Who do you think you're fooling?" she scoffed. "You know he's dead or you wouldn't be sniffing around. Never saw any relatives, or friends of relatives, here before. I suppose it's the house you're after. Well it's my bet that he left it to one of those young men of his, not that they'll live long to enjoy it if he gave them what he had! Serves them right, that's what I say."

"Fuck you," is what I said in reply.

I dropped the china off at a charity shop on the Caledonian Road and headed back south via Tavasso's deli and the wine shop, to Shoreditch. These terraced houses were unlikely to ever have a Volvo sitting outside, not unless it had been pinched. Still, as I pulled the lock over the steering wheel I hoped that my luck here would be better than it had been in Kentish Town. One way of attempting to trace Connie Smith would be to ring every Smith in the phone book; not completely impossible but, let's face it, life is short. What I'd try first was simply asking if anyone in the street knew anything about her. People are usually helpful, although you do need to be convincing. Years ago I found an enormous box of yellowed stationery in a junk shop and I make use of this fairly often. Using a fountain pen I write an address, supposedly that of my mother, on the front of the envelope, and the name of the person I'm looking for and their old address on the back. Sometimes, just for the fun of it, I cannibalize my brother's old album for a stamp. If I can't be bothered to do this I simply rip off that corner. X last wrote from this address, I say, waving the envelope as proof. X used to be a good friend of my Mum's, and she's anxious to get back in contact. Before you get your envelope out, however, it is important to check that your Mum's supposed friend really isn't still in residence.

"Connie Smith?" He was a big man, over six feet and solid with it. "Well I'm blowed, fancy asking for Connie Smith!"

"Do you know her?" This was looking promising. "She lived here twenty-five years ago."

"And still does." He laughed, "She's my missus. I'm Laurie Emanuel and she's been Connie Emanuel now for twenty years." Holding out his hand he said, "Connie's out shopping but can I help you, pet?"

Brilliant. Shoving the redundant envelope back in my pocket I shook his hand and explained I was looking for someone Connie had once worked with. The name Perry Alms didn't mean anything to him, but he assured me that Connie would help if she could. I asked for their phone number and said I'd return the next afternoon, if that was convenient.

"Give us a buzz first but I expect we'll be in. Tell me though, this Perry geezer, what do you want with him?"

Laurie's manner was friendly enough but in this part of London there's no chance of getting any information out of anyone if they suspect the police, or any government bodies, are involved.

"Don't worry," I said, "this isn't anything official. I'm working for a solicitor who's trying to trace the relatives of an elderly woman in Australia who died recently. I think there's quite a lot involved."

"Really?" His broad face cleared. "Well I'm more than happy to do someone a good turn. Lucky blighter, I hope you find him."

Turning on Lucy's radio, I sang all the way back to the flat.

By nine o'clock that night we'd finished the first course. "What do you think?" Fran whispered to me in the kitchen. I thought her new glasses were a mistake and that Doc Martens with leggings didn't do much for anyone past puberty. Fran's enquiry, however, didn't pertain to herself.

"A darn sight better than the wrestler." I searched for a coffee filter.

"Tor, she might have been a horrible mistake, but she wasn't a wrestler! You won't say anything about her in front of Suzanna, will you?"

"Don't be silly, of course I won't."

Fran's mistake reminded me too much of one of my own, a doctor named Harriet whom I'd pursued solely on the grounds that she seemed hard to get. Harriet used to say G.P. didn't stand for General Practitioner but for Great Person and at the time — these were my salad days, mind you — I'd thought that was incredibly funny. I'd lusted after her for weeks and the lust was eventually reciprocated as the result of a late-night pub crawl. A couple of hours later I'd realized that Genuine Pervert was closer to the truth. A little make-believe bondage with a couple of silk scarves, or the belt off your dressing gown, is one thing; wet leather straps and handcuffs are something else. It had been a one-night stand with Harriet doing all the standing; over me at one dreadful stage, holding something that she assured me was a genuine branding iron which she knew how to use. I believed her. Completely. It had been an experience which had left me literally tied in knots, and badly frightened.

"These are sweet." Fran held up one of a set of yellow and black coffee cups that April had washed earlier in the afternoon.

"Mmm. April likes them."

"And you do like her, don't you? Suzanna I mean."

I nudged her toward the living room. "She's totally delicious."

She was also alarmingly predatory. "A private detective? That sounds fascinating!" April and Fran were sitting at the dining table, carving the *pain forte* into slices.

"It is!" April cheerfully called across the room, unaware that a seduction was being attempted on the scatter cushions. Somewhere along the line I'd kicked my shoes off, and was now regretting it. Suzanna had shed her strappy silver numbers as well and although I kept edging sideways her toes were managing to keep up with mine. Any moment now she was going to be in my lap.

"Have a look at this." April went over to the bookshelf for the photo of the vase. I hadn't actually meant to take the photo from Bry's desk but had picked it up along with the photos of Perry and the pages from the address book. While April explained to Suzanna how valuable the vase was, and how I was looking for its twin, I took the opportunity to abandon the floor for the sofa.

"Very nice." Suzanna's green eyes plunged straight into mine. Jesus, she was actually crawling across the floor toward me. It was like being stalked by a big cat. "Here," she growled, "take this." She held the photo up, leaning a generous breast against my knee as she did so. She wasn't wearing a bra and beneath her ivory silk shirt I could see that her other breast was pleasantly heavy, the nipple erect.

By now April was watching. "So." She stepped around Suzanna and plonked herself down on the sofa beside me. "You and Fran are off to Paris in the morning?"

Giving a lazy laugh Suzanna shook tangled black hair out of her face and sat back on her heels. "Yes, I'm going to some auctions, and Fran is going to take herself around the museums."

"It's terribly romantic!" Fran giggled from the other side of the room.

"Oh, terribly." April agreed. "I can see that."

"I did not fancy her!" I protested later. "Not really. It's just that no one's made a pass like that at me for ages."

"You were looking at her tits, I saw you."

"It was difficult not to, one of them had taken up residence on my knee."

"She's going to ring you, you know that."

I stretched out on the bed and gave this some thought. "I think you're right. I think she'll ring me at work and suggest a drink or something."

"Well I can guess what the 'or something' will be."

I quite enjoyed April in jealous mode but didn't want it to go too far. "Fran is what worries me, she thinks this is True Love, plus joining the dating agency cost her a lot of money. She's in for a big disappointment."

"Victoria." April was standing in front of me. "Are you sure you didn't fancy her?"

I pulled her down onto the bed. "I didn't want to do this to her, if that's what you mean. She had nice tits, my love, but they didn't make me want to do this."

Sunday morning we slept in, then drove back to Battersea, collecting Gareth from Will and Jen's new flat on the way. While April prepared lunch Gareth and I donned scarves and gloves and went for a wander around Battersea Park. As usual we finished up staring through the wire mesh at Fred, the albino wallaby.

"Are you sure he's happy here?" A new note of skepticism had entered Gareth's voice.

"Fred? Sure I'm sure. I mean being an albino wallaby in Australia can't be much fun can it? Think how sunburnt he'd get."

Gareth looked dubious; Fred just looked dead miserable.

After lunch I left mother and son channel-hopping between old black and white movies and drove back through the almost-deserted city, heading across Clerkenwell and Finsbury up to Shoreditch.

"Those were the days." Connie Emanuel, née Smith, threw back her head and gave a throaty laugh.

Her husband looked at her fondly then tossed a wink across at me. "The best looker in Mayfair she was. I used to watch her going past and think 'Oh, I'd like a bit of that!' All the other birds were skin and bones, I could never see the point. That Twiggy, for instance, she was half starved. I like a woman with a bit of flesh on her."

Connie had lots of that, and it suited her. She was a big woman with a big smile. "I fainted into his arms, right outside the club I was working in. I'd been dieting, trying to keep up with my mates, and I was that weak I could hardly stand up. I came to and there was this big feller holding me in his arms, and when I told him what was wrong he was that mad! 'You bloody fool,' he said. 'You're bloody beautiful the way you are!' "

They'd got married and Laurie had moved in. The T.V. Smith in the phone book had been Connie's dad, who'd died some years back.

"Bry Rocke," Connie reminisced, "I remember her all right. She and Charlie were a right pair of lovebirds, and talk about party! I'd leave the club at dawn and they'd still be at it."

My story was that Perry might be able to claim from an inheritance and that I'd contacted Bry Rocke in order to trace people he'd worked with. "I'd help you if I could," Connie said, "but I didn't see Perry again after he left B-Rocke's. Why Bry said I was a particular friend of his I don't know, I mean I got on with him, he was a nice bloke, a real gentleman in fact. But I didn't know much about him. Never went round to his place or saw him outside the club."

"Do you know what interests he had?" I asked.

Laurie's interests were no secret; the walls were covered with photos of boxers and darts championships. He saw me looking and grinned.

"That's my life, up on the wall, and in that chair over there." He nodded at Connie. "How's about a cuppa then, Vicky?"

I winced and said please. He headed out to the kitchen.

Connie tried to remember what she and Perry used to talk about, then sighed and gave up. "You know I don't think we talked about anything, really. Well we talked about the club of course, but not about anything personal. I knew he was queer, but it was never a subject of conversation. A lot of the boys who worked at B-Rocke's were that way inclined, Charlie and Bry thought they created a better atmosphere, and we used to have a great old time gossiping about who fancied who. But I can't imagine Perry ever unbending that much. Not that he was snooty, but he was private. Dressed nice, quiet but nice. I do remember thinking he must have had some private money because of the way he dressed, and because he always caught a taxi. I'd walk from the Bond Street Tube but he arrived in a taxi every night, and that's how he went home too. Never saw him walk anywhere."

"Do you know where home was?"

She frowned. "Do you know I think it was near Harrods? Because he once said something about going to their food hall for a certain sort of biscuit he liked and that stuck in my mind. I'd never been in Harrods, I thought it was all posh clothes and I didn't even know they had a food hall."

"Can you think of anyone else who worked at the

club who might have known more about him? Bry mentioned a barman named Paul Brown."

Connie smiled up at Laurie as he brought in a tray. "I can't say I remember anyone of that name, but it's twenty-five years ago and there were people coming and going all the time. Things were never really the same after Bry and Charlie went down to Brighton, we all missed them but it was getting too much for Charlie. He'd start gasping for breath sometimes, and his lips would go a kind of blue. He couldn't keep on the way he'd been going, that was for certain. And then the coppers would turn up and there'd be a ruckus."

"Did the police turn up often?"

She reached for a biscuit. "Pretty often, but we were used to it. Mum never liked it, mind, she wanted me to work round here in a day job, serving fish and chips somewhere where she could keep an eye on me. Fat chance there was of that! I was all for a bit of excitement."

"It's not the same now." Laurie settled into his chair. "I know things got a bit rough, but it was nothing compared to what goes on now. Villains wasn't just villains then, but part of the community. The old people could talk to them if they had a problem. And if a woman's husband died, or if he was inside, someone would organize a whip around to help with the rent, or they'd come up with a radio or even a telly. Now they'd get raped, and have the telly nicked."

"What about the kid sister?" Connie asked. "Perry often used to have a long natter with her, she might have more of an idea of what happened to him."

"Perry had a sister?"

"No!" Connie laughed, "Bry's sister, Louise. She used to hang around the place at one time. She was a funny one, not like Bry at all."

I left a little later, with Connie apologizing for not being able to help and Laurie inviting me back anytime I was passing. As I was wrestling with the steering lock Connie ran out and knocked on the window. "I've just had a thought. There is a bloke who might be able to tell you something. He used to work round the clubs doing a bit of this and that, tending the bar or doing the door. I ran into him a couple of years back in a record shop in Notting Hill, along Ladbroke Grove I think it was. He's well into his fifties and calls himself Ted-the-Man." She rolled her eyes. "Anyone would know who you mean because he's a Sixties freak, still dresses in all the gear and has long hair. He told me he'd got scrap albums and cuttings from those days, and he seemed to know about people I'd forgotten completely. He's the only person I can think of."

"Great, thanks. I'll see if I can find him."

She blew warm air into her hands. "Well, watch him if you do, love, because he's not a nice piece of work. In fact I wouldn't mention him to you if I didn't think you could look after yourself. He used to like the young ones, the teeny boppers who'd hang around the clubs, trying to sneak in. I heard tell he'd let them in if they went round the back with him first."

"A real charmer."

"A real arsehole," she said. "You watch yourself with him, all right?"

* * * * *

66

I didn't sleep well that night. I started off by thinking about Suzanna, which made me worry about Fran. From worrying about Fran's future I moved on to my own, beginning with the flat and ending with personal pensions. I was paying into a personal pension scheme, but the amount I was putting aside wasn't about to buy me a very comfortable old age. I could probably scrape together a bit more each month but what if I'd invested in a company that went bust? What would happen if the whole market collapsed, or the fund managers did a Robert Maxwell and scarpered with the loot?

In the end I overslept and only just managed to get into the office for a ten o'clock appointment. Anchee pulled a face and then agreed to make a strong coffee for me and tea, with two sugars, for Mrs. Grainger, a witness I was interviewing for a solicitor. Mrs. Grainger was in her late forties, with cheeks the color of strawberry jam and eyes like blue buttons. She worked as a cleaner in a City bank and on her way home one morning had witnessed an assault at Charing Cross Tube.

"So tell me," I said, stifling a yawn. "What exactly happened?"

"Well he walked up behind this young woman, picked her off the ground and threw her on the tracks."

"Good God." The solicitor's details hadn't arrived and I'd been expecting nothing more than a drunken brawl, or a snatched wallet.

"Two or three people rushed forward to pull her back onto the platform but no one did anything about him and I thought to myself, he's a lunatic, he'll do it again and next time there might be a train coming. There were lots of strapping big men in suits standing around, so I yelled that we should hold onto him. Not one of them budged, they either looked away or shook their heads. Well I wasn't having that."

To be honest I'm not sure that in a similar situation I'd rush to help either; my first instinct would be to call the police. "What did you do?"

"I tackled him of course." She was all of five-foot-three, maybe four. "He was a whopping big bloke, mind you, but I grabbed hold of his right arm. Well, he started punching out, yelling obscenities, but I held on all the same. He landed a punch on my right ear and I saw lights and thought this is it then, but all of a sudden a young colored man came and helped me. By this stage the big man's shirt was half off and there was blood everywhere. As soon as they saw that, of course, no one else would come near us."

"Whose blood was this?" I spoke into the cassette player. "Was it yours, Mrs. Grainger?"

"No love, it was all his. He had these bloody great cuts going all the way up his arms, didn't he? When the police eventually turned up we could see that he'd taken a razor blade to himself, and then stitched the cuts with cotton; but struggling with us all the stitches burst. I came home looking like I'd spent the day in an abattoir."

As I showed Mrs. Grainger out, Anchee said Joyce, the genealogist, had rung. On Saturday afternoon I'd left a message on Joyce's answer machine, asking her to do an urgent check through the past six months' death certificates for Paul Brown. Anchee said Joyce hadn't found a death certificate for a Paul

Brown of that address, and that she was still working on Perry Alms.

Not dead after all, Mrs. King.

Back in my office I rang Mark Young. Mark was the younger brother of my friend Phoebe and worked as a social worker at an AIDS helpline.

"Hi there Tor!" he bellowed into the phone; in the background was a radio, and behind that office noises. "How you doing? Got a phone call from Pheebes last week to say she and Malcolm are going to tie the knot. They need to make it official if she's going to stay in New Zealand."

"That's totally brilliant!" Phoebe had met Malcolm at the same Oxford party where I'd met April. "Give her my love, won't you? I will get around to writing one day."

"I'll tell her. Now what can I do for you, Tor?"

I told him and he promised to get back to me. I brought my notebook up to date, told Anchee I'd see her tomorrow morning, then caught the Tube to Ladbroke Grove. The search was on for Ted-the-Man.

CHAPTER SEVEN

"Who?" The display he was rearranging consisted solely of compact discs. Was I the only person in London who didn't have a CD player? What was wrong with cassettes anyway?

"Ted," I repeated. This was the third shop I'd tried.

"Yeah, but Ted who?" He pushed up the sleeves of his Guns 'N Roses sweatshirt.

I couldn't bring myself to ask for Ted-the-Man. "I

don't know his last name, but he's really into the Sixties."

"Oh yeah? Well there's no one here like that." He turned his back and started unrolling a large poster.

"He was working in a record shop on this road a couple of years ago."

"Oh yeah?" He spoke over his shoulder, "He's never worked here, that's all I can tell you."

I was the only customer in the cafe next door, which was a pity because they did a nice line in buttered toast and hot, strong tea. I rationed myself to one cup as it wasn't the sort of establishment that ran to a loo for the customers. The waitress was about my age and looked as if she'd worked there for a while. "Cold out there isn't it?" She shivered.

"Freezing. I've been walking up and down, looking for someone who works, or used to work, in one of the record shops."

"Oh yeah?" This phrase was obviously local dialect.

"A guy named Ted, a couple of years ago he was working along here. He's an aging Sixties fan, still has long hair."

She pointed out the window. "You could try up there."

"Where?"

Her hand cleared a path through the steam. "See? Second-hand records, up there on the first floor. They might be able to help."

"Thanks." My kidneys really weren't what they used to be. "Could I possibly use your loo?"

She smiled sympathetically. "Through the curtain at the back, love. It's the weather that does it. That and the tea."

Ten minutes later I pushed open a purple door and was greeted by a blast of Jimi Hendrix.

"Wow!" I managed.

"Loud eh?" He was about eighteen and on the verge of deaf, if the volume was anything to judge by.

"Yes," I yelled back. "It's loud all right."

He reached out and turned a knob. "Don't worry, I was only testing."

My ears had taken on a high-pitched ring. "I like Hendrix but can't take those decibels."

"The man was unreal." He nodded sagely. "Like, out of sight." Something told me I'd come to the right place. I had.

"Ted, yeah that'd be Ted-the-Man. I know him."

"That's great, can you tell me where he lives?"

He looked me up and down, "I guess it's cool, you don't look like the fuzz or nothing." He scribbled a phone number and a local address.

"Do you know what his surname is?" I asked. "I just know him as Ted."

"That's right," he nodded. "Ted-the-Man."

Notting Hill, during the Sixties, was the preserve of bohemia and hippiedom. Since then there have been waves of recolonization, first by punks, then by yuppies. From the state of the linoleum in the hallway, however, it was obvious that the yuppies hadn't made it this far.

I knocked on the door of Ted's first-floor flat and an elderly man poked his head out from a door further down. "He ain't in. And she ain't there either. Did you see those loose banisters on your way up?"

There was a smell of brussel sprouts and cooking and scorched cloth. "No, I didn't notice any. I wonder if —"

"That's the problem, people don't notice. There'll be a death here one day, mark my words. I've told the landlord but no one listens to me. Bloody Jews. They own London now, do the yids. Lose a war and win a country."

It was a novel view of history. "Do you know when Ted will be home?"

Pulling a handkerchief out of a trouser pocket, he blew his nose. "You can never tell, though lately they've been in most nights, smoking their *ganja*. They say it's incense but I can tell the bloody difference." He peered at me from behind the handkerchief. "Come to buy some, have yer?"

This wasn't a conversation I needed to get into. "Thanks for your help, I'll call back some other time."

"Bloody addicts." The handkerchief disappeared again. "Why don't yer just bugger off?"

I made it back to Hoxton just ahead of the rush hour. The red light was blipping on the answer machine and the first message was from Joyce, saying that she'd actually started the search on Perry Alms on Friday afternoon, and had been able to finish it today. She'd checked both birth, and death, certificates, and found that he'd been born Peregrine Louis Alms in 1943 in Lightwater, Surrey.

Not far from where I was born myself. His parents were Louis William, and Catherine Anne, née Austin. His father had been a major in the army. Joyce said things had been quieter than usual at St. Catherine's and so she'd also done a quick check for siblings over a ten-year period, but hadn't come up with any. She hadn't come up with a death certificate either. She'd put an invoice, for sixty pounds, in the post.

The next message was from Denise, the friend who was going to rent the flat from me when I moved out. She'd next be down from Manchester on Wednesday afternoon. The final message was from Mark Young. "Hello there Tor." His voice had taken on the self-consciously wooden tone most people adopt for answering machines. "I've got the information you wanted. You're right, Paul Brown's in an AIDS hospice, pretty ill by the sound of it." There followed the hospice address and phone number.

Not dead but, by the sound of it, dying.

I piled a plate with risotto straight from the fridge, decorated it with glops of tomato ketchup, then collapsed onto the sofa. The fact that Joyce hadn't turned up a death certificate for Perry Alms didn't rule out the possibility that he'd changed his name by deed poll and subsequently died, or that he'd died overseas and that the death hadn't been registered with the British consulate. But I'd work on the premise that he was still alive and kicking.

So what next? The hospice, and another visit to Ted. I found myself checking my watch; it was only six o'clock. I hadn't got much sleep last night and was tired. I checked my watch again: it was still six. I needed to go to the loo, clean my teeth, and apply another layer of lip gloss. Fifteen minutes, I could be out of here in fifteen minutes. It took twenty.

The hospice was in Muswell Hill, a large Victorian building which might possibly have been described as handsome by daylight but at night was merely bleak. The ambience inside, however, was warm and friendly. The reception desk was ablaze with chrysanthemums, and the receptionist, who was in the process of arranging the flowers in metal vases, was helpful.

"Oh no," she said, shredding leaves with practiced fingers before crushing the ends of the stems, "we're very relaxed here and don't worry too much about set visiting hours. But I will check with the ward if you don't mind, to make sure Mr. Brown is up to seeing you at the moment."

After being given the go-ahead I followed the corridor along to the end then turned right.

Paul Brown wasn't the first person I'd seen with AIDS but it still came as a shock that a man in his forties could be so ravaged.

"Hello there." The woman who stood to greet me was in her early twenties with skin that was pale to the point of luminous and red hair that cascaded in waves to her waist. If it weren't for the fact that she was wearing flowered summer shorts over a black leotard, along with boots designed for a building site, she might have stepped out of a

Pre-Raphaelite painting. Her handshake was firm. "Are you the person Mark was making enquiries for today?"

"Yes, I'm Tor Cross."

"This is Paul, and I'm his buddy, Lyn. I've only just got here myself, I was worried Paul would think I'd got lost." A faint accent indicated she'd spent some time in the States.

"Not you." His grip on her wrist looked stronger than I would have expected. "I don't worry about you getting lost, ever."

On the bedside table were red roses in a vase and a card with a little girl in a pink dress saying, "Thinking of you!" Shit. Turning up like this verged on the ghoulish.

"I'm sorry," I apologized to both of them. "The reason I'm here is because I'm looking for someone you used to know, Paul, someone you worked with years ago. But if you don't feel like talking to me I quite understand. I don't want to worry you at all."

"Sit down, please." He waved me into a chair. "I'm not dead yet and I like meeting new people."

I didn't come up with any concoctions about lost inheritances but simply said that I was looking for Perry Alms, who used to work at B-Rocke's in Mayfair.

Paul looked at Lyn. "It's like what we were talking about the other day."

She leaned slightly forward. "How do you mean?"

"Synchronicity, that's the word you used, isn't it? For the way a thing, or a person, suddenly keeps getting mentioned, even though you mightn't have thought about them for years." This speech evidently tired him and he closed his eyes for a moment.

Lyn rubbed his left hand between hers. "That's right, Carl Jung had theories about it. Is this Perry someone you've recently been thinking about?"

"Yes." His voice was brittle. "I haven't seen Perry Alms since he left B-Rocke's. I hadn't thought about him for a long time, until a few days ago." He turned his head on the pillow and gave me a faint smile. "I was thinking that Perry was probably the only person I've met who really believed in God. You see I was wishing that I did too."

After leaving Paul and Lyn, the last thing I felt like doing was driving to Notting Hill to see if Ted-the-Man was at home, but I went all the same.

Ted's neighbor had been right. A couple of the banisters were distinctly wobbly and the smell of patchouli came with an undertone of dope.

"Well hello." Ted's face was pockmarked and there was a graying, wispy beard to match the hair tied back in a ponytail. "We were just sitting here, talking about dead ladies, and here you are." If I hadn't disliked him so much on first sight I would have burst into tears. Instead I let myself be led inside.

"You like black light, do you?" She was fifteen, maybe, with a gold nose stud, bloodshot eyes edged with black, and a long dress in crushed green velvet. Without the cluster of spots under her bottom lip she could be the latest in a line of supermodels: post-modernist waif. The worn carpet was scattered with posters burned into an ultraviolet mess of purples and oranges.

"I haven't seen anything like that in a long time," I said.

The look she gave me asked where I'd been.

Ted was picking the posters up, moving across the room in slow motion. "You ask me what art is and I say this." He hoisted one into the air like a flag. "Am I right, Cho?" he quizzed the girl.

"He's right," Cho announced.

I couldn't imagine her saying anything else. What I wanted to say, however, was that he was all wrong. I wanted to bundle her out the door and a long way from here. But there was something about Cho that suggested she'd seen worse than Ted-the-Man. Besides, what did I have to offer as an alternative? London was full of kids like this and tonight many of them would be sleeping out in doorways or under bridges. People like me gave them a fifty-pence piece when they begged from us, but we didn't take them home and give them chicken soup and a place to sleep.

"This is my favorite." Cho pointed to a picture of two naked women sprawled on top of each other, trickles of blood running from their wrists. The dead ladies, I assumed.

"She's morbid, that's what she is. Aren't you?" He pinched her chin. "You're a morbid little girl. And you —" Letting go of Cho he stood too close for comfort. "What are you?"

Jesus, this guy was a jerk. "I'm someone who's interested in the past." Hopefully this sounded esoteric enough to make up for the disappointment of my not being a customer. "In the Sixties. I'm trying to trace someone you might have known in the Sixties."

He hung a lazy arm around the girl, who compliantly sagged against him. "And who told you to come here?"

"Oh, a few people. I've been asking around and your name kept coming up. I'm trying to find a man named Perry Alms, he used to work at a Mayfair club called B-Rocke's."

Ted gave me a slow grin. "You know lady, I think you've come to the right place."

The posters were all stowed on a table in the corner, the lights were back to normal and Ted and I were sitting on a greasy sofa in front of an electric fire. Cho had been sent out to the kitchen to fetch coffee. My host was affability itself.

"Now Perry." Ted shook his head. "He was someone you know, a real gent was Perry."

"Did you know him well?" From the little I did know about Perry, Ted didn't seem a likely friend.

He nodded. "Pretty well, yeah."

I didn't believe him, but I didn't know why he'd be lying either.

"He left B-Rocke's in 'Sixty-nine, but I don't know where he went after that."

I was wearing the blue suit I'd bought in Brighton, and Ted's demeanor slipped for a moment as he made it obvious he was ogling my knees. What was this? I was years past my sell-by date as far as he was concerned. Gritting my teeth I crossed my legs. The skirt rode up even higher.

His teeth were stained yellow. "Do you mind telling me what this is all about?"

As Connie Emanuel had said, an arsehole. "Not at all. He's a distant cousin of my mother's. A great-aunt has left some money in her will to me, and to Perry, but the solicitor has told me I can't have my share until Perry has been traced."

"Is that right? Must be quite a bit of money if you're going to all this trouble."

Concentrate Tor, that was a stupid story to have used. I attempted to back-pedal. "It's not much really but I've been unemployed for a year so anything helps."

"What's in it for me then, if I can tell you where he is? A hundred maybe?" He tugged at his beard and pushed his right thigh against mine.

I wanted to gouge his eyes out; I wanted to knee him in the balls. "If you can tell me where he is I think fifty's fair."

He agreed immediately, which I hadn't expected. "I don't mind admitting I could do with fifty quid. You know, I seem to remember that Perry wrote to me after he left. Yes, that's right. I always keep letters, I never throw anything like that away. Look, why don't I have a look now?"

He got up and left the room. Cho came back in with a mug of coffee that I had no intention of drinking.

"Thanks." As I took the mug I noticed her fingernails were chewed to the quick. "By the way I like your dress," I said. "The green matches your eyes."

The eyes in question widened. "Wow, people never seem to notice that, that my eyes are green."

"Oh they probably do, they just don't mention it. Green eyes are unusual, especially as dark as yours."

"Unusual, do you think so?" This was pitifully easy, she was so desperate for attention. I was about to say something about her hair when Ted came back in.

He shook his head. "I know I can find it but it'll take me a while. But look, I came across two albums of newspaper cuttings that might interest you. See that?" He opened one of them. "That's Esmerelda's Barn. Talk about wild! None of today's clubs has what it takes. These should be worth twenty for a loan, don't you think?"

What the fuck did I want with his poxy albums? I was being conned, we both knew it. His voice was wheedling. "Twenty for the albums, and for me racking my brains over the next couple of days. But they're only on loan mind, you'd have to promise to bring them back. And when you do I'm sure I'll be able to tell you where Perry lives."

It wasn't as if there was anything else offering. "Fine," I said. "And thanks." From across the room Cho gave me a funny look.

I was back home by eleven and there were two messages on the machine. Pushing the playback button I heard April say she was going to bed early, if I wasn't in by ten she'd talk to me tomorrow. Denise had rung again to announce she'd be arriving on Wednesday morning, rather than afternoon. She couldn't remember where she'd put the key I'd given her, but she was bound to find it so I wasn't to worry if I wasn't planning on being around. And I wasn't to worry about Wednesday's dinner either,

81

she'd take care of it. I assumed that meant she'd be staying for a few days. I rang Bry Rocke.

From the sound of it the call was being taken in the bar. A male voice said someone would find Bry, and shortly afterward she answered from her office. "Ms. Cross, how are you?"

Tired was how I was. Tired and grubby and depressed. The only positive thing I had to report was that Perry Alms didn't seem to have died in the last twenty-five years. Not in this country at least. I said I hadn't been able to locate Ray the car dealer, but I had spoken to Connie, and to Paul Brown who was seriously ill and in a hospice. Bry hesitated when she heard that and then asked for the hospice address, saying she'd send a card. She couldn't remember anyone named Ted Mann but I very much doubted he'd given me his real name: I certainly hadn't given him mine. Ted had said he was going away for a few days and had insisted I take his number so I could ring and arrange a time to bring back the albums. I avoided supplying my number in return by claiming that I'd just moved and the phone wasn't connected. He'd known it was a lie and I'd known he'd known. At least it was clear where we all stood.

"So what happens next?" Bry asked.

Good question. I pondered it for a moment then decided not to answer on the grounds that what I had in mind wasn't strictly legal. It's not always a great idea to fill your clients in on every detail.

"There are a few avenues yet to explore," I said. "But I'd like to think about them for a while if you don't mind. I'll let you know as soon as anything comes up though, Bry, you don't have to worry about that."

Her laugh was understanding. "Whatever you think, Tor. By the way, I was looking through my address book again this afternoon and I've come up with another name, Florence Litton. Flo was one of the cleaners at the club and she's in my book because she sometimes 'did' for me at home too. I can't think why I didn't think of Flo the other day because Perry took a special interest in her. He was always very kind to her and I remember that they seemed to know each other from outside B-Rocke's. The problem is, she'd be well into her seventies by now. Flo lived in Balham; you know, Gateway to the South. No phone listing but I've got the address."

"A Balham address?"

"That's right." She coughed. "Excuse me. Yes, downtown subtopia. Balham, Tooting, they were pretty rough areas when I lived in London but I believe things have improved since those days. I went to a party south of the river about five years ago, some people I know bought a big house in Clapham. I thought they must be mad when they told me, but when I got there it was quite civilized."

"Oh everyone's moving southside these days," I said airily. "You'd be surprised."

After giving me Flo Litton's address Bry asked if I'd taken her photo of the vase.

"Sorry Bry, I picked it up by mistake. Do you need it back straight away?" There was a stain on the carpet where Fran had spilled red wine on Saturday night; I'd have to get some carpet shampoo.

"No, but I would appreciate it if you didn't show

it to anyone, I feel nervous about people knowing what I've got stashed in my safe!"

"Don't worry, I won't." I didn't see Suzanna as a potential safe-cracker. I was about to ring off but then remembered something Connie had said. "One last thing, have you asked Louise about Perry?"

"Louise?" This was said like she was trying to think who I could mean. Louise, I mentally gave her a prod. Your sister Louise, a woman on a veranda.

"Why should I ask Louise?"

"Connie remembered her being at the club and said that Perry used to talk to her."

"Oh no," Bry dismissed this. "Louise was as much in the dark about where Perry had gone as everyone else. There's no point in asking Louise, no point at all."

That night I dreamed about Paul Brown. He was dancing, wearing a long rainbow-colored jacket, and the girl he was dancing with had Lyn's flaming hair and eyes like Cho's. As they swung past they smiled and waved. Behind them were Fadia and her mother from the hotel; they too were smiling and waving. When I woke up I couldn't remember if I'd waved or not.

PART TWO

PART TWO

CHAPTER EIGHT

Steph was back.

"You've got a tan!" I accused her.

She pulled the front of her sweater down to reveal cleavage the color of warm honey. "This goes all the way down to my painted toenails."

"Never!" For me, cleavage was out of the question, but why couldn't I have a tan? All I needed was a case that would take me to warmer climes, where I could laze by the edge of a hotel pool . . .

"Hold on," I said, "you were supposed to be

sweltering in a hired car, following your quarry around Caracas." Not only had she had time to paint her toenails, she'd done her fingernails too. And hennaed her mane of hair.

This was greeted by a dazzling smile. "I didn't get the run-around we anticipated. In fact Mrs. Gillespie invited me in and gave me her full cooperation. The reason she'd played at being such a hardarse in the past was because she was still furious with her ex, but now she's found someone else and doesn't give a toss about the divorce going through. Mission accomplished. I rang Gerald, the solicitor, and he was over the moon. He said the hotel room was a package deal, booked for a week, so why didn't I stay there and enjoy myself? Which is exactly what I did." She opened her wide mouth in an even wider yawn.

The last foreign job I'd had involved me spending a week in a seedy hotel in Athens, unable to speak the language, unable to locate the man I needed to interview, and eventually succumbing to terrible diarrhea. Steph, however, would never find herself in this uncomfortable position because she is, quite simply, the luckiest person I've ever met.

Yawn finished, she put her head to one side. "So how have things been here on the factory floor?"

"Oh you know how it is." I swung my foot at an imaginary beach ball. "January's always dead slow."

After enduring ten minutes of Steph on Caracas nightspots I went back to my office and rang Sarah.

"What are you doing home?" I asked. "You're never home. I was looking forward to a chat with your machine."

"I've got a cold." She snuffled rudely to prove it.

"So if you're after someone to hang around on street corners you can think again."

"Have I ever asked you to do that?"

Sarah and I seemed to be seeing each other less frequently and I sometimes suspected the reason for this was that she didn't really like April.

"Huh!" she snorted, "because of you I've rubbed shoulders with skinheads, dealers, all the best company."

These are social groups that I'm not particularly good with. Sarah, however, has a flair for this sort of work, as well as a wide range of contacts.

"You don't have to leave your armchair for this one, I promise. I'm chasing a missing person and getting nowhere fast."

"They're the worst." She gave two loud sneezes. "Excuse me. There's nothing worse than searching for someone who has a serious interest in not being found."

How serious was Perry Alms, I wondered? Serious enough to really go missing? Serious enough to change his name and identity? Because if he'd gone that far I wouldn't have a hope of finding him. And would he have gone to all that trouble because of a vase that the owner hadn't missed for over twenty years?

"That was a loud sigh," Sarah said.

"Sorry, I was just thinking. As I said, I'm getting nowhere and I was wondering if you might have a friend who could check vehicle licenses for me." Connie had said Alms always took a taxi. Maybe a man who didn't like to walk had learned to drive.

"You want a bent copper."

"I do. For twenty quid I want a copper bent

enough to check licenses for me, and for another twenty I'd like a check on convictions." The vase incident apart, Perry didn't sound the criminal type. But a gay man can get himself a record without trying too hard.

"A license check costs thirty these days, while previous records, that'll be another thirty."

Plus thirty to Sarah for her trouble, call it a hundred.

"Deal. By the way, when am I going to see you again?"

"Funny you should ask 'cos Lea DeLaria's coming back to town and I thought I'd get us tickets."

Lea De who? A few years back Sarah had dragged me along to watch Karen Finley, who I'd thought was both terrifying and brilliant. "If this involves nudity and disgusting acts performed with chocolate cake you can count me in."

"Tor! Lea DeLaria is a comedian. You must have heard of her, she's the one who does jokes about Hillary Clinton."

I thought we thought Hillary was a good thing. "But we like Hillary, don't we?"

The explosion at the other end was part laugh, part choking fit. "Yes we do like Hillary, that's the whole fucking point. You know what you are? You're a cultural illiterate, you have absolutely no feel for the zeitgeist."

"That's not fair, it's just that I've been very busy lately."

"Yeah, like for the last ten years. Hey Tor, you heard the news? k.d. lang is a l-l-l-l-l-librarian!"

Shit, I thought after hanging up, maybe Sarah was right. I'd have to start buying *Time Out* again.

I'd agreed to help Diane with an insurance surveillance during the afternoon and as we left the office we crossed paths with Gerald, the solicitor, who'd arrived in order to whisk our star off to a celebratory lunch at the *Poule à Pot*. The last time Steph had lunched at the *Poule* she'd sworn that Princess Di had been at a corner table, wearing sunglasses and a strawberry silk catsuit. I've never caught sight of any of the royals anywhere I've eaten, and none of my clients has ever offered to wine and dine me at a French restaurant. I guess I'm just not the French restaurant type.

After waiting two and a half hours in the freezing cold, Diane and I got photos of her man climbing over a side fence and jogging to the corner betting shop — which wasn't bad for someone crippled by a bad back. I then dropped her off at the agency and headed straight down to Battersea to collect April. We were combining my Balham enquiries with a visit to our future home.

The house was in cream-painted brick, at the end of a terrace. "Sorry about the mess." The current owner wrestled with a lively toddler, whose vocabulary extended to one word, "Mine!"

"Not yours!" She retrieved my leather glove for

me. "Sorry about the teeth marks. Look, just wander where you will. I know what it's like when you're moving, it's difficult visualizing how your own furniture will fit in. Do you want me to leave some curtains?" This was addressed to April. I don't quite know how she categorized me, presumably as friend-cum-lodger.

I left them discussing curtains and carpets and went through to the kitchen, which had been the selling point for me. The room was a good twenty feet long by about twelve feet wide, with red quarry tiles on the floor, whitewashed walls, a porcelain butler's sink and handmade cupboards with wooden doors. The effect was country farmhouse, and I liked it enormously. At the moment there was a large oak dining table in the middle of the room but April and I intended to get something in scrubbed pine, when we could afford it. The back door led into a medium-sized, pleasant garden and I'd been pleased to find a mat of juniper in the far corner. There'd been a poem I'd come across at school, something about juniper and a girl holding a bracelet to the moon, and I tried now to remember who'd written it. Was it Laurie Lee? Images from the poem, sexual and disturbing, had accompanied me through adolescence.

"You still like it?" April's hand was on my shoulder.

"Yes!" I wanted to swirl her around the room, bracelets jangling, the moon agog.

"Funny that it's the kitchen you like so much, when cooking isn't your favorite occupation." Before following April upstairs I unlocked the back door and peered out into the garden.

"Gareth's going to love his bedroom, don't you think?"

"He liked it as soon as he saw it, especially the wallpaper. And the light shade, I hope she's going to leave that." We were back in the car and I was checking the *A-Z*.

"The second reception room has a nice feel to it."

"I like it best, after the kitchen." What I particularly liked was its limed wooden floor, which would look good with my Ikea rug and white bookshelves.

"Yes, I think I'll turn it into a guest room, second television room."

"Oh." Let's face it, at the moment I was the lodger. What rights did I have, with no share, as yet, in the mortgage? I suddenly felt extremely peeved. Why was April taking these unilateral decisions? Maybe I wasn't even the lodger, with a lodger's rights, maybe I was simply a guest, with no rights whatsoever. Maybe I'd be better off staying in my own flat.

"Tor?" Her hand was on my knee. I closed the map, switched off the inside light and turned on the engine. "You do like the house don't you?" Her voice was small in the dark.

A girl holding a bracelet. "Yes." I leaned over and rubbed her cheek with mine. "I adore the house, and I adore you."

April settled down with a thermos of coffee, a blanket and a book, and I knocked at the door of what had been Flo Litton's abode twenty-five years ago.

"What do you want?" She peered suspiciously

around the chain. Bry had said she'd be in her seventies.

"I'm sorry to bother you, but I'm looking for a Mrs. Litton."

The chain remained in place. "No one here by that name."

Drat. "She lived here in the Sixties, she was a friend of my mother's." I fished in my pocket for the all-important envelope. "See? Here's the address on the back. I'm trying..."

"I've lived here ten years and I don't know nothing about her." The door slammed shut.

Standing at the front gate I gazed up at a sky faintly sprinkled with stars, not a sight you often see in London. One down, how many to go? Three houses further along the terrace I had more luck.

"Florence Litton, that's right." She had a pleasant Kingston accent. "I knew her daughters, Mary and Bridget. The family moved, oh it must be fifteen years now, you know."

"Can you remember where they moved to? Or do you know anyone else who might still be in contact with them?"

"I don't know where they went but I can tell you someone who does."

"Great, who's that?"

She gave a big grin. "My sister Beverley, she stayed in touch with the youngest, Bridget. If you wait a minute I'll write Bev's phone number down for you. Bev lives close by, in Streatham, but she'll be away till late Sunday night."

* * * * *

"Got it?" April threw the blanket into the back seat.

"Well I got something. I thought you were reading a law book?" On her lap was one of Ted's albums.

"It's wonderful, the clothes, and the hair!" Her seatbelt clicked into place. "And all the nightclub gossip of course. It's fascinating, Tor, you must take a look."

"I'd be more enthusiastic if I hadn't had to fork out twenty quid for the experience."

"But not your twenty quid, it's not out of your pocket."

It was easy for April to be pragmatic; she hadn't met Ted.

I spent the night with April in Battersea then drove back to Hoxton. Saying that she thought she'd be able to find the key was Denise-speak meaning she'd lost it, so I'd have to wait in. I binned this morning's junk mail, hid the latest Visa bill in the bottom drawer of my desk, then curled up on the sofa with a bowl of toasted muesli.

Not for much longer, I thought, looking around the living room. Oh no, I was going to live in a house with juniper in the garden. On the brass card table under the window a carved bird my brother had sent from Australia lifted its beak to the ceiling, uncomfortable and out of place in this room. Next to it the hand-painted hanging, from Kenya, was similarly ill at ease. The truth was I'd just never been able to get this flat together. The ancient leather sofa I was sitting on had been wonderful in the Camden flat Alicia and I had shared; here it was the wrong size, the wrong color. In even the tiniest of my undergraduate rooms the kangaroo vine on the top bookshelf had looked luxuriant and full of light; in this room it created its own dark corner. Giving up on the whys and wherefores of this I put the muesli bowl on the floor and opened the smaller of Ted's albums.

The clothes were, indeed, a hoot. And the hairdos, how did it all stay piled on top? The album's cuttings were predominantly about music and pop groups and I'd just started reading about a legal battle in the record industry, involving a soloist whose name wasn't familiar at all, when the doorbell rang. Looking out the window I expected to see Denise on the doorstep, suitcase in hand. Denise, however, wasn't on the doorstep, and there was no sign of a suitcase. Instead she was opening the doors of a large van. When she saw me she waved wildly; I mightn't have moved out yet, but Denise was moving in.

The driver of the van was Rosie, a strapping twenty-year-old who, so she informed me, usually did this for a living but was today doing Denise a favor. "Everything's dandy." Rosie grinned at me. "But it's been a long drive so I'll have a five-minute breather. Then I'll get that back room cleared for you." Pulling a crumpled copy of *Viz* out of the pocket of her tweed jacket she settled down into the sofa.

I retreated to the kitchen in order to take stock of the situation and make some strong filter coffee.

By the time I'd regained my equanimity Denise was sitting on a cushion on the floor, making a call to the owner of the van, and Rosie had abandoned *Viz* in favor of the second of Ted's albums.

"You don't mind do you?" I didn't mind Rosie reading the album but I did resent the fact that she was smoking in my flat. I handed her a mug of coffee then headed back out to the kitchen in search of a makeshift ashtray. On my return she was jabbing a nicotine-stained finger at one of the clippings. "I'm sure it's them!" She thrust the album into my hands, "It is them, isn't it?"

"Who?" I presented her with an old saucer then turned the album the right way up. The picture she was so excited about was of a group of revelers holding champagne glasses. The headline read, *Much Ado About New Mayfair Hot Spot.*

"Them!" Holding the saucer in her left hand she pointed at two men in suits. I thought I'd seen them before too, but I couldn't think who they were. Actors maybe? I didn't recognize the other man, or the young woman next to him.

"I'd bet anything that's Reg and Ron!" Rosie pulled the album in her direction. "See, it says, A well-known duo help new club owners . . . Hey!"

I'd hauled the album back. ". . . help new club owners Charlie Heatton and Bry Rocke celebrate the opening of their swish Mayfair club, B-Rocke's!" Pushing past a startled Rosie I carried the album to the window and studied the picture. Yes, it was, it was Bry, with a beehive hairdo and pancake make-up. Charlie looked a good bit older than Bry. The men with them were slightly out of focus so it was impossible to be sure, although I thought Rosie was right, they did indeed look very much like Reg and Ronnie Kray, London's notorious gangster twins.

Rosie knew everything there was to know about them, or so she informed us over a lunch of cheese and chutney sandwiches. "Have you seen the film, *The Krays*? Gary and Martin Kemp were fantastic. You ought to read the books too, *Our Story*, you've just gotta read that, and Reg's book, *Born Fighter*. You know it's tragic really, the stuff about being in prison all these years, and their Mum dying. They've done loads of work for charity. I think they should be let out."

I offered her some chorizo. "No thanks, I'm a vegetarian, I don't believe in killing animals. I went on the big demonstration you know, to mark the twenty-fifth anniversary."

I don't eat much meat myself, but I do have a weakness for salami. "What demonstration was that? The Animal Liberation Front?"

Rosie's eyes rolled. "The demonstration about releasing the Krays!"

"It was twenty-five years ago that they went to jail?" Things were getting curioser and curioser. "They were sent down in 'sixty-nine?"

"That's right." Rosie gave a sober nod. "In May. It was springtime, which makes it even sadder. I think Reg has written a poem about it, or maybe it was Ron."

Immediately after lunch I rang the paper where my friend Jan worked and left a message asking her to get back to me as soon as possible. Then I settled down with the album while Denise and Rosie hauled furniture.

My eyes ran over the various headlines. *Carnaby, the Most Famous Street in the World!* This was the London of my childhood. In the playground at primary school we'd worn fluorescent orange hearts pinned to our chests and wept in simulated anguish over Paul or Ringo. *Swinging Like a Pendulum!* Down in leafy Surrey, time had moved slowly, and London had been a different world, a throbbing, paisley world ruled by defiant teenagers with long hair. "Peace!" we'd screamed out of the bus windows every morning but none of us knew what that was about and although I longed to one day join the ranks of the teenage army I also found the prospect a mite daunting.

In my subteens the London I knew from television and magazines was inhabited by pop stars in impossibly tight jeans and models in impossibly short skirts. Our parents didn't approve and that was recommendation enough. Cockney lads set up shops that exploded overnight into business empires, and students defiantly squatted in luxury flats left vacant by wealthy Arabs, or American film stars.

The London in Ted's album had another side to it as well. The first clipping was from 1959, an interview from the *Daily Sketch* with a man who called himself King Olivia and professed to be the head of two gangs. He declared his intention of eventually taking control of all the nightclubs around the West End. At the top of the clipping someone, presumably Ted, had scrawled *Jo Olivia shoots his mouth off!* The next article was from February in

1960 and concerned a shooting in a club called The Pen Club, near Spitalfields Market. There followed similar accounts of shootings, stabbings and trials, and then on the fourth page a gossip-column article about Reginald and Ronald Kray and their popular nightspots, the Kentucky Club in Mile End Road and Esmerelda's Barn in Knightsbridge.

A few pages further on, Charlie Heatton, well-known clubber and nightclub owner, was mentioned in a list of guests at another club owner's fortieth birthday party. And then, three pages after that, an item on a Miss Bryton Rocke, fiancée of Charlie Heatton, nightclub owner, who had been acquitted on charges of passing stolen checks.

Well, well. That rustling in the branches overhead must be the Cheshire Cat, about to disappear into its own grin.

A photograph showed a jubilant Miss Rocke and friends celebrating her acquittal on the steps outside the law court. Bry was wearing an ankle-length mink coat. Charlie, resplendent in a white suit and broad-rimmed hat, had his arm around her shoulders while immediately behind the happy pair a man in dark glasses and a smart jacket looked remarkably like Reggie Kray. At the top of the article was a cryptic hand-written comment, *The Kite-Flyers Congress!*

I reached for the phone and tried Jan again.

"Hello Tor, I was about to get back to you. How's things?" From the sound of it she was eating a late lunch.

How were things? I contemplated Bry's face as

she laughed into the camera. "I'm not sure, to tell you the truth. Let's just say things are interesting."

"Interesting for me too?" Jan was a journalist through to the marrow.

"Sorry, but probably not. Jan, am I right in remembering that you were doing some research a few months ago on London gangs after the war?"

She burped without apologizing. "Me and every other journalist in town, gangland is currently in."

"Is this because of the Krays and the twenty-fifth anniversary?"

"Shit, where's the lettuce? There was supposed to be tomato *and* lettuce." There was a pause and then she went on. "The Krays? Well yes, they're part of it, everyone's milking the Kray story for all it's worth. Plus, there's a general air of nostalgia for old-fashioned thuggery. Why do you ask?"

"Because a case I'm working on goes back to the Sixties. Look, I know it's short notice, but could we meet for lunch?"

"Like when? My fingers are walking through my diary as we speak."

The Kite-Flyers, what were they I wondered? "Like tomorrow?"

"Oh." Knowing Jan, her fingers were probably in the middle of next month. "Well I can in fact, but it will have to be late, I'm busy till after one."

"Could you make two?"

"Can't see why not. If something does come up I'll ring. At Gino's?" Jan taxis around town on an expense account so she's usually happy to meet wherever it's most convenient for the other party.

"Please. And one last question, in your research have you ever come across a group known as the Kite-Flyers?"

There was a pause. "Not that I can remember, although I've come across the term *kite-flying*."

"What's it mean?"

"It's crim slang for passing checks that are forged or stolen. A lot of it used to go on in the Fifties and Sixties, on a highly organized basis. It still does, although credit card fraud has really taken over."

"Thank you," I said. "And see you tomorrow."

Three hours later I'd read a whole range of articles about an amazing array of West End clubs, illegal casinos, discothéques, brothels and strip joints. Interspersed with various knifings, robberies and not a few murders. I'd also come up with half a dozen references to Bry and/or Charlie, including an article about the latter being taken to court over a pearl-handled revolver which the police had stumbled across in his office during a raid on the club ten months after it had opened. Charlie's defense had been that he'd been looking after it for a wealthy patron, who'd left it with him one night after having too much to drink. "He said he was scared he might do his wife if he took it home. I thought the safest thing was to lock the gun away in my office." Rumor had it that the patron concerned was a member of the House of Lords; Charlie, however, refused to name names and the jury had demonstrated its approval by finding him not guilty. The judge had expressed some surprise. It wasn't explained why the club had been raided in the first place.

In another piece, about West End clubs raising money for an old people's home, Perry Alms, the manager of B-Rocke's, handed a check over to a smiling priest. Perry looked much the same as he did in the photos Bry had given me.

The album's last few pages covered the early months of 1969. There were cuttings from *Sunday People* about clubs and pornography rings in Soho, and then a couple of front pages from newspapers, dated the 10th of May, announcing the arrest of the Krays. Following these were two articles about an illegal casino and then, on the last page, a small, torn cutting about a birthday celebrated in the famous strip club, Raymond's Revue Bar. A businessman wearing a party hat, and looking extremely drunk, sat next to his wife, who also appeared to be somewhat the worse for wear. The guests seemed to be a fairly motley crew, but at the end of the table a pair of men caught my eye. There were two reasons for this. Number one, they looked sober; two, one of the men was Perry Alms. Perry was described as "the popular manager of B-Rocke's nightclub"; the black man with him wasn't named. Like Perry, he was in his mid or late twenties, and was smartly dressed. Something about the way they almost, but not quite, leaned into each other made it clear they were an item; the wide band each wore on the third finger of his left hand suggested they'd been together for some time.

After dinner Denise went off to have a bath and April rang to let me know that the woman from Balham had been on the phone to say she was leaving more curtains than she'd offered last night.

"And the light in Gareth's room? I know it's not a big deal but there were planes on it and he seemed quite taken." When I was Gareth's age I'd had a pink lightshade, with yellow horses, that I'd been immensely proud of.

"I didn't want to ask, in case it sounded greedy. After all, she doesn't have to leave anything."

As soon as I put the phone down it rang again. It was Fran, and the news wasn't good.

"The trip to Paris was wretched, Suzanna was horrible. What's wrong with me, Tor? Why does it always turn out like this?"

"It doesn't. You lived with Joan for seven years and that was a stable relationship. Joan was normal." Albeit extremely boring.

"She still left me though, didn't she?"

I was more interested in hearing what form Suzanna's horribleness had taken. "She struck me as a bit moody," I offered.

"Moody? Bad-tempered beyond belief. When she wasn't at an auction, all she wanted to do was go to expensive shoe shops. She's an art specialist for Christ's sake! I thought we'd go to the Louvre and some of the galleries but when I suggested that, all she did was sneer. She even intimated she'd find me a whole lot more interesting if I was on Prozac. Well fuck her, that's all I can say."

"How did you leave things? Did you have a final argument or not?"

Fran faltered, "Well, no, I didn't feel I could say too much because she was paying. But if she ever rings again I'll tell her what a cow she is."

"I didn't like her, you know."

"But you said you did!"

"I was lying, you seemed so smitten. She simply wasn't good enough for you, Fran."

"Oh. Well I wish you'd told me what you really thought. I was very hopeful about Suzanna, you know."

"I know." I glanced up at the mantelpiece, where Denise had pushed my glass paperweights aside to make room for a collection of porcelain figurines. Denise, I asked myself, would Fran get on with Denise? Two of the figurines were shepherdesses, complete with sheep. Probably not.

"Denise has moved in," I said. "You would not believe how full this place is of bric-a-brac. As for the kitchen, we've got four of everything."

"That reminds me, you know the photo of the vase April showed Suzanna? Well, she said it wasn't worth anything like what you'd been told."

"Oh? Well I think it's only immensely valuable as one of a pair."

The stuff Denise had spread around the room really was amazing. Where had she got those blue plastic candlesticks from for instance? And why?

"Suzanna said vases like that don't come in pairs, and they're only worth two or three thousand pounds at the most. I hate to admit it Tor, but I think when it comes to antiques she does know what she's talking about. Anyway, she also claimed to have seen that particular photo before, about six months ago in a copy of *Antiques*. She remembered it because she'd done a lot of business with the dealer who was selling the vase; he'd taken out a full-page advertisement and asked her what she thought of the layout."

A small metal vase, photographed against a lime-green wall. Could this be true? "If that's true, why didn't Suzanna say something when she saw the photo here?" As I asked I knew the answer. In a day or so I'd be getting a call from Miss Suzanna: her bombshell about the vase would provide her with an excuse for ringing.

"I asked her why she hadn't said anything and she replied that if you wanted to believe a cock-and-bull story, that was your problem. She really is a bitch, isn't she?"

"She sure is. Did she say anything else about the dealer, Fran? Do you know what his name was?"

"She didn't say. But she did say his shop was in Brighton."

CHAPTER NINE

At nine-thirty the next morning I was rifling through dusty cardboard boxes in Mr. Rabin's exceedingly chilly storeroom.

"Any luck yet?" He peered round the door.

"So far all I've come across is back copies of *The Tatler.*"

"The customers expect it." The face he pulled was apologetic. "If I am selling a beautiful mahogany side table they want to see it scattered with these magazines. Why wealthy people want to read about

Euro-trash is beyond my comprehension. But I know the copies of *Antiques* are there, Victoria, at least two boxes." He clapped his hands together for warmth. "I will bring you an electric heater, and a cup of tea. Or coffee? With you I am never sure which."

Mr. Rabin had called on my services four years ago, when he was worried he might have bought stolen goods, and after I allayed his fears we'd stayed in touch. In his early seventies, he always wore black trousers with embroidered braces, and starched white shirts with the same pair of gold cufflinks. One night he'd cooked me dinner in his tiny flat and rolled his sleeve up to reveal the number tattooed along his left forearm. Bitterness? No! The soup ladle had danced in the air. One must never give in to bitterness; giving in to bitterness meant giving in to fascism. But he did admit to bad dreams.

I eventually located the magazines and twenty minutes later had found the photo of the vase. The asking price was two and a half thousand pounds.

I carried the magazine through to the shop. "That's what I was after."

His lips pursed. "I have never been interested in such objects. My interest is in tables and chairs, where people get on with the business of life. Beds too, but beds take up too much space in the shop." He laughed. "You are moving house, Victoria, can I interest you in a beautiful oak bed, very old, with lots of happy memories?"

* * * * *

"You forget your brolley?" Anchee asked.

I was soaking. "With your powers of detection you really should give up on the typing and hit those streets. I brought Lucy along today and there was nowhere close to park."

Her smile was self-congratulatory. "Well that problem might end soon, I've been negotiating with the feminist publishers on the corner for a couple of parking spaces out back."

"If you pull that off you're a genius." Alicia's approaches over the years had got her nowhere.

After drying my hair off with a teatowel I rang the Brighton antique shop and asked for the owner by name. He'd had some ormolu ornaments in the July advertisement and I claimed it was ormolu I was interested in.

"It's a pity you didn't ring a few months back, I had some nice pieces. But do keep in touch, it is something I look out for."

"Thanks, I will. Someone I know suggested you, he said you'd been recommended to him by a woman named Bry Rocke."

"Bry is one of my most favorite people! She's always giving me good references."

"It's nice to have friends one can count on."

When Bry had needed a photo that would be convincing she'd known whom to ask. I thought back to when she'd shown the photo to me, at a point in the conversation when I was looking doubtful. It was like my scam with the envelopes: seeing is believing. And it had worked; I had believed her.

* * * * *

"The lasagna I think, how about you?" Jan put down her menu.

I hadn't picked mine up. "Gino can read minds, he knows what I want."

The pat he gave me on the back of the hand was part friendship, part rebuke. "Veetoria will have the sardines. I keep saying, try something different, my menu has more than one thing to offer, but she refuses."

"It's true," I said, "I'm a creature of habit. Are we drinking or not, Jan? If you want we can order a half-carafe of the house wine."

"I'll stick to mineral water, I've got a lot to do this afternoon. What are we starting with, business or gossip?"

"Let's begin with gossip. Business will require a clear deck."

After we'd emptied our plates, Paola, Gino's Neapolitan wife, brought over two cappuccinos and a plate of chocolates, then helpfully cleared a space so Jan could open the album. She put on her reading glasses and spent a good five minutes browsing. "This would have saved me a few hours in the library. Very interesting Tor — now what is it you want to know?"

"I want to know what you think about the compilation as a whole. And then I'd like to ask about three particular individuals."

She frowned down at a stray thread on her green linen jacket. "As I said, the album's interesting; a history of clubland, or if you prefer, gangland London through much of the Sixties. There was a period when clubland and gangland were almost synonymous. It's a nice collection too, someone had an eye for the main stories. And from some of the comments written in, it's obvious they knew who was who and what was going on."

"That's what I thought. Right, the individuals I'm concerned with are a woman named Bry Rocke and her lover Charlie Heatton, they owned a club in Mayfair called B-Rocke's. The manager of the club was Perry Alms. Do these names ring any bells?"

"None at all."

"What about Ted Mann, aka Ted-the-Man? This is his album."

She shook her head again and I pulled my chair round and flipped to the end of the album and the picture of Perry and his companion. "Here's Perry Alms. And here —" I'd marked the article about the club's opening with a yellow post-it, "— are Bry and Charlie."

"Love the makeup! How did those eyelashes ever stay on?"

"These days she runs a club in Brighton and does a nice line in sequins."

"So this is who you're working for? She must be getting on."

"She was pretty young in the Sixties and now is well-preserved. And this is all confidential and off the record, okay?" She nodded uninterestedly and I continued. "Right, here's Bry again, celebrating on the court steps with friends. The flash geezer in the glasses, does he look familiar?"

Jan peered at the photograph. "I know who it looks like, it looks like one of the Kray boys, but I wouldn't swear to it."

"Have another look at the second picture again, those two on the right."

"They do look a bit like the twins, but once again it's hard to tell." The glance she gave me through the glasses was interested but wary. "What's this got to do with the Krays, Tor?"

"I don't know if what I'm working on has anything to do with the Krays, but it seems that Bry knew them, and she's asked me to trace Perry Alms, who disappeared from view in May of 'Sixty-nine, at about the same time that the Krays were nicked."

Jan performed tailor's pleats with her napkin. " 'Sixty-nine really was the end of one era and the beginning of another. The swinging Sixties ending, yet at the same time Armstrong and Aldrin landed on the moon, and Prince Charles was made Prince of Wales. Northern Ireland reared its head too, of course, with the army taking over police and security."

She stopped pleating. "Do you still get nervous about traveling on the Tube, or is it just me? I sat all the way from Bond Street to Bank yesterday, staring at a gray jacket that had been left on the seat opposite and wondering if there was a bomb underneath. And then I thought it didn't matter anyway because I'd be in the center of the blast and would never know what hit me."

Before I could reply she slapped herself soundly on both cheeks. "This is not a subject I want to discuss. You work in London, them's the risks. In the Seventies it was platform heels — today it's terrorism. Back to the Krays. When their empire toppled I suspect a few people did absent themselves, either for fear of being implicated, or because they were terrified of being dragged along as witnesses. It's also possible a few might have been concerned lest they finish up at the bottom of the Thames, complete with cement shoes. This is all speculation on my part ... but your man Perry, disappearing at the same time — well, that might simply be a coincidence mightn't it? Do you know if he was involved in any funny business? Why is it that your lady of the sequins wants to find him after all this time, anyway?"

I'd managed to comb the froth on my coffee into a perfect curl. "I have no idea. She spun me a line which has turned out to be complete crap."

"Which makes you nervous, right?"

"Not necessarily." I put the spoon down. "I'm used to my clients lying to me. Very often they only tell you part of the story, or they change some of the details in order to make themselves look better, or they consider it's no business of yours anyway and spin you a yarn. It usually becomes apparent early on and then they come clean and you wonder why they didn't tell the prosaic truth in the first place. What does make me hesitate here is the possible link with organized crime, even if it is now ancient history."

Jan peeled the foil from a chocolate. "These are scrummy. I must say, if it was me I'd want to know exactly what was going on. I'm aware we're in different lines of business but I couldn't take working in the dark, and although all this stuff happened a long time ago it isn't impossible that people out there are still interested in revenge and retribution. But something you should also keep in mind, Tor, is that times have changed. London, God knows, has changed. In the Sixties the boundaries between criminals and fashionable society were very blurred, it was fashionable to rub shoulders with hoodlums in dark suits. The Krays were wined and dined by film stars and minor aristocrats and more than one politician. They were the bad boys everyone loved to love, they gave money to charity for Chrissake! Reading the lists of the rich and famous who frequented their clubs is like going through *Who's Who* — even Judy Garland sent Reggie a telegram when he got married. You know something else?" She touched my wrist.

"What's that?"

"We would have been there too, sister. You and me. Esmerelda's Barn was the swingingest place in town. I would have bopped the night away and come back with stories about hunky Mafia types in dark glasses, and how Ron Kray brought in his pet donkey, wearing a hat. And you'd have told lurid tales about the goings-on in the basement."

I felt slightly disgruntled. "So what am I doing in the basement while you're upstairs mixing with the toffs?"

"Tor, I know dykedom is fashionable these days, but it wasn't invented in the Nineties. Downstairs was a lesbian club. The Krays were extremely violent, not averse to killing people, but the one thing they could not be accused of was homophobia."

Gino brought over the bill and I nabbed it. "This is on me. Jan, you are a mine of useful information. Though I find the donkey a bit hard to believe."

"Cross my heart. A donkey was nothing in those days. Exotic pets were all the rage, you could wander into Harrods and buy yourself a cute little lion. Pop stars strutted along the King's Road with tiger cubs on leashes. I remember begging my parents to let me have a boa constrictor because I had asthma and couldn't keep a cat."

I got back to the agency to find Nigel had sent over another batch of mismatched signatures. After working on these I drove home via my local Co-op, where luxury items were noticeably absent from the shelves but it was possible to stock up on the basics. April and I ate toast and scrambled eggs in front of the Channel Four news, then she sat down with a law book and I rang Brighton for the second time that day. My client was in her office.

"Hello there Tor! I was hoping you'd ring." Her tone was more urgent than her words but I'd made up my mind during lunch that I wasn't going any further with this case unless Ms. Rocke provided some explanations. And I didn't want to give her the opportunity to think up a new story.

"I've got some possible leads but I do need to see you Bry. We have to discuss where to go from here, and there's a photo I want to show you. It's of Perry with a man who appears to be his lover. I'm hoping you might recognize him. How about I come down tomorrow night?" And while we were discussing Perry and friend, maybe we could chat about some other matters. Kite flying for example, now that would be an interesting subject. And how about those lads in the dark glasses, were they Kray lookalikes or the real thing?

"Of course." But her voice was disappointed, she'd obviously been hoping for more. "However the afternoon would actually be better for me. We've got a big-deal birthday party booked for tomorrow night and I'll be tearing my hair out over whether or not the cake has the right number of candles. I'm always here on Fridays from three because that's when I do the books. Can you make that?"

As far as I knew, all Anchee had me down for was a morning interview. "I can, I'll talk to you then Bry, I'm expecting a call from someone else right now." I wasn't interested in prolonged discussion at this moment.

"I'll look forward to it, it'll be good to see you. And thank you Tor, I do appreciate what you're doing for me."

Hanging up, I thought that her tone had seemed oddly affectionate — and wistful.

CHAPTER TEN

Mr. Stone's daughter escorted her father up the stairs to the office then disappeared to check out some sales. I hoped she wasn't taking advantage. Five minutes with Mr. Stone and I knew she was.

"What happened then, Mr. Stone?" My ankles were twisting round each other. Every time I attempted to untwist them the interview would take a turn for the worse.

"What happened then? Why then the red car drove straight into the back of the other one."

"Do you know what color the lights were at the time?"

"They were red." He nodded.

"How can you be sure of that?"

"I remember I thought, that's funny, when the car kept going. I thought, that car should have stopped."

"So you'd seen the light was red?"

"Not really." He tapped the side of his nose. "I've never seen a red light Miss, if you know what I mean."

Spare me. "I'm sorry, but I don't know."

"Color blind of course! I've never seen the color red in my entire life. But I can tell when the traffic lights change." He leaned forward. "I've developed a sixth sense."

My ankles took on a life of their own. "You said you saw the red car hit the other one. How did you know the car was red, Mr. Stone?"

"I was talking to someone at the time and I heard a loud bang and the man I was talking to said, 'look at that, the red car drove straight into the back of the other one.'"

I pressed the pause button on the cassette player. "So you didn't actually see it happen?"

"Didn't have to, you could hear it all along the street."

As Mr. Stone's daughter hurriedly ushered him out Anchee put through a call.

"Hello Tor," someone said, meaningfully. "This is Suzanna. Has anybody ever told you that you have very, very sexy feet?"

Just my luck, being propositioned by a foot fetishist. If I told any of my friends they wouldn't think it was exciting, they'd think it was hilarious. I hesitated. Should I begin by pointing out that I was a married woman? Or with the fact that I thought she'd treated Fran despicably? Inspiration flashed. "You make my toes curl Suzanna. And that isn't meant as a compliment." I dropped the receiver back into its cradle: Brighton, here I come.

A few miles past Hayward's Heath it began to snow and by the time the train pulled into Brighton Station there were regular flurries. I intended to treat myself to lunch at one of the old-fashioned hotels on the seafront and asked the taxi driver to drop me off next to the Palace Pier. Hugging my coat, I stood with my back braced against the rails and looked along the length of the seafront, where snow swirled in different directions. Immediately across the road a grand Regency hotel had all its lights on and two small faces pressed against one of the first floor windows, children watching snow fall over the sea. One of them waved and I waved back.

By the time I'd finished lunch the flakes were heavy and falling with more determination and there wasn't a taxi to be seen. Pulling my shawl up from under my collar I covered my hair and struggled up Old Steine into the town center, where I walked into the first shoe shop I saw.

"You don't have to tell me." The assistant glanced at my light leather shoes and indicated I should take a seat. "Madam requires a pair of wellingtons."

I'd lost my last pair during a somewhat riotous picnic in Richmond Park. "Madam does."

He held up a pink plastic number, with a fake fur lining, and I shook my head. "Mud-green will do, in size forty please."

"Try a forty-one." He handed me a pair. "So you can wear a pair of thick socks. We do a nice line in chunky, natural wool."

I pushed my feet in. "I guess this weather is wonderful for business."

"Actually it's not because wellies are relatively cheap. Strappy, high-heeled numbers for summer, now that's what turns a shoe salesman on." He blew a kiss into the air but his fervor was wasted on me. Suzanna, no doubt, would have understood.

I set a good pace in my sensible footwear and arrived at B-Rocke's with a few minutes to spare. Shallow footsteps in the snow led along the back street to the club's side entrance so I took it that Bry was in and I wasn't going to have to hang around in the blizzard. I rang the buzzer but at the same time noticed the door wasn't on the catch; pushing it open I stepped inside.

"Bry? I'm here!" I stamped soundly on the mat then walked across to the door that led into the club proper. Only one overhead light was on and the room looked smaller than it had the other night. The black lacquered chairs were upside down on the tables and there was a strong smell of floor polish.

I called again, more loudly. "Bry, this is Tor!" I was a bit early so maybe she was somewhere in the building where she hadn't been able to hear the buzzer. Cutting across the dance floor I opened a door under a green Exit sign and peered down a long, dark hallway. At the far end I could make out an open door; halfway along, Bry's office door was shut but light came from underneath.

"Bry, I'm here!" Bry didn't answer.

Taking off my gloves I ran my right hand down the walls but couldn't find a switch. It was at about this stage that I felt a familiar pattern of goosebumps beginning: the hairs on my forearms began to prickle, my woolen tights started to itch, my scalp tingled. "Shit," I muttered under my breath. And then, "Bloody hell."

What needs to be explained here is that I have a problem, not always but sometimes, with long hallways, dark or not. On some occasions I'm absolutely fine; other times I get spooked. This was not the sort of phobia you'd want to offer to Diane for interpretation, but as far as I could remember it went back to when I was ten and Ma sold the house where Tim and I had been born, and where our father had died, in order to buy a bigger house in a better street. In between houses we spent two months in a rented flat, and the only thing I can remember about this interim period is that I got scared every time I had to walk down the hall to my bedroom. In fact I couldn't walk down it, I had to run. My cat, Otto, felt the same. This afternoon, however, I didn't want to run down this hall; I simply didn't want to go down it at all.

I rapped my knuckles impatiently against the door frame. A childhood phrase floated to the surface: "Knock, knock!" This was becoming ridiculous. Taking a deep breath I walked purposefully along to Bry's door and with a sweaty palm turned the doorknob.

She wasn't there. But she couldn't be far away because from the radio on top of the filing cabinet the Pet Shop Boys were singing their cover version of "Go West," and on the desk the computer screen was covered with columns of green figures. I dumped both my bags on the floor and my coat and shawl on a chair.

Stepping back out into the hall I kept my eyes on the door at the far end and walked quickly toward it. The door pushed open on a small room with blue wallpaper, a parquet floor and a polished wooden table with a vase of white roses in the center. To my left a door padded with red leather was half open, and from behind it came the sound of another radio. I gave the leather a firm push with my fingertips and it swung on oiled hinges.

Windowless royal blue walls were hung with faded tapestries, ornate mirrors, hunting scenes in gilt frames. At the end of the long room was a well-stocked bar with carved wooden paneling and fluted columns; from the ceiling a tiered chandelier threw a rainbow around the upper walls.

I had the strong feeling I wasn't meant to be in this room.

Some of this feeling was undoubtedly due to the fact that beneath the chandelier sat an enormous roulette table. It wasn't too hard to deduce that I'd walked into an illegal casino. What worried me more than this deduction was that at the other end of the roulette table a heavy chair had fallen over, and on the floor next to the chair the radio also lay on its side. Something about the angle of the chair . . .

"Bry? Hey!" I yelped as a crash came from out in

the hallway, the crash followed by running footsteps. Then silence.

I instinctively crouched down behind a chair, and stayed frozen that way for a couple of minutes, trying to still my breathing and watching the doorway.

Breathe in; one, two, three. Out; one, two, three. They've gone. Somebody had been out there, but now they've gone.

And then what do you do? No, you don't stand up and move toward the door; you don't force yourself to walk back down that hallway. Not yet. Because what you have to do before you do anything else is turn your head. You turn your head and you look under the table, in the direction of the toppled chair.

Bry Rocke looks back. Her eyes are wide, and thick red blood oozes from her left nostril, pooling under her left cheek. Her mouth is slightly open and between painted lips her tongue is a thin wedge of the palest pink.

CHAPTER ELEVEN

Fumbling in his pocket the young plainclothes policeman pulled out a handful of tissues. "Whew Chief! What's that?"

"That" was where I'd thrown up over the aspidistra.

Inspector Vann ignored him. "You're not used to discovering bodies in your line of work, are you Miss Cross? I guess it's mainly divorce work you do, tracking down errant husbands. Now I take it that this is your coat?"

"I don't do divorce work."

"No?" He handed my coat and scarf to the police surgeon who shook out the scarf then quickly ran her hands over the coat. A policewoman had checked my shoulder bag and was now inspecting the plastic Marks and Spencers' carrier containing Ted's album.

"No, I don't do divorces." It seemed important that he should understand this.

The Inspector looked down at me and nodded thoughtfully. "I'm glad to hear that, it's a mucky business. Now if you go to the station someone will take a full statement from you. I'll be along in a while."

Out in the hallway people were arriving with camcorders, cameras and lights. A man in a white laboratory coat walked past, with an armful of folded polythene bags. The policewoman handed me my things. "Let's go," she said. She'd seen this all before. "It's getting too damned crowded around here."

Two detectives, a woman and a man, interviewed me and then Vann arrived and we went through it all again. My credentials had been checked and no one, at this stage anyway, seemed to suspect that I might be the guilty party.

"Do you know what I think?" Vann had thick, silvery hair and wore a tartan bow tie, which he tugged at every so often. This was the first policeman I'd seen wearing a bow tie, and although there are some tall men in the force I'd never come across one as tall as he: six-foot-eight at least. "Twenty years in this job has convinced me that luck does exist. Some people are lucky and you're one of them. My guess is, if you'd arrived five minutes earlier you would have ended up dead too."

It appeared that the murderer must have heard me calling and hidden in the broom closet. The crash I'd heard had been a metal bucket falling out into the hall.

My story about how Bry had employed me to look for Perry Alms didn't interest the Inspector as much as I'd expected and I had the definite feeling that he knew why Bry had been shot, if not who had done it. I was asked to stay in Brighton overnight, in case I was needed again in the morning, and a room was booked for me at the Albion, where I'd had lunch.

"You're not tee-total are you?" Vann asked as I stood up to leave.

"No."

For today's interview with Bry I'd donned a severe black wool dress with long sleeves and narrow satin cuffs. As I pulled the left cuff down under my coat I could feel that something had dried around the edge. I hoped it was nothing worse than my own vomit.

"Good. Now what you need to do is have a small brandy as soon as you arrive at the hotel. Call dinner up to your room, watch something mindless on the box, and then have a hot shower. Have another small brandy before you go to bed, it'll help fight the shock. But only small ones, remember. If you have too much to drink tonight you'll be dogged by nightmares for the next fortnight. I know, because I've had it happen."

Under different circumstances I would have found him unbearably patronizing; right now he was fatherly, and I appreciated it.

"Thanks for the advice."

"And don't forget to ring your boyfriend and tell him where you are, we don't want a missing persons being put out on you on top of everything else."

As I got into one police car I saw Louise up ahead, stepping into another. "A relative," my driver informed me. "Off to the morgue to identify the body." As we drove past, Louise's face was white against her scarlet coat. I managed a small wave, but she didn't see me.

As soon as I got into my hotel room I rinsed my cuff under the hot tap, without looking, then had that first brandy. After that I rang April and cried.

Although it had snowed heavily during the night, at nine the next morning the sky was a brilliant blue and there wasn't a cloud to be seen. I pulled the heavy socks over my tights, shoved my feet into the wellingtons, took my scarf and coat from the wardrobe and went downstairs. At the reception desk I was told that Inspector Vann had rung and said it was fine if I wanted to go back to London, but would I please inform him if I was planning to be absent from my usual address for more than a day or two? There was also another message, from Mrs. Iris Rocke, Bryton Rocke's mother. Mrs. Rocke would be very grateful if I could ring her back as soon as possible. I shoved Mrs. Rocke's phone number into my coat pocket, put on my gloves, then walked down the steps and out into the snow.

There are actually two piers in Brighton, though the west one is derelict and closed to the public. Turning in its direction I walked along the King's

Road seafront. A number of other people were doing the same and on one bench a family was break-fasting with thermoses of hot tea and Mars Bars. "Morning!" the parents chirped at me in unison while their blond offspring crammed chocolate into their mouths so as to leave their hands free for snowballs.

"Beautiful isn't it?" The woman gestured toward the beach with her steaming mug. Her cheeks were ruddy.

I looked out over the sea. "Yes. It is."

"Have you seen him yet?" The oldest boy gave me an intense look with slate-colored eyes. "See? He's coming again!"

I held my hand up against the glare and there was a speedboat towing a wet-suited skier. With the blue sea and sky as background, and the glittering snow as foreground, we could have been basking in Florida. Nowhere else but England, I thought. The thought was curiously comforting.

Mrs. Rocke's secretary, Joseph, was short, gray-suited and reticent. The Rolls-Royce he was driving was in classic black and we crunched in comfort along a private drive until we came to the Georgian sandstone building that was Mrs. Rocke's private residence. I'd guessed Bry's background was secure; this was sumptuous.

"Miss Cross, thank you so much for coming."

As she greeted me I was reminded of another elegant, older woman on whom I had so recently served a writ — but where Fadia's mother's eyes were tired as the result of what they'd seen, Iris Rocke's glittered. And where one woman bowed to fate, the other deferred to God.

"God's ways are beyond our knowing," she said, "but it is some consolation to me to think that my daughter was saved from what might have been a very painful death. The Inspector assures me that she died instantly. Under the circumstances I consider this a blessing."

The circumstances were that Bry Rocke had had cancer and had recently been told she might have only a year to live. Three years ago she'd had a partial mastectomy, followed by a complete hysterectomy.

"The doctors had offered her further treatment but didn't pretend that they could provide her with much more time, or an improved quality of life. After thinking the matter over she had decided not to proceed with any drugs other than painkillers. She wished to die with as much dignity as possible."

Bry's death hadn't looked very dignified to me, but it had undoubtedly been quick.

Joseph appeared with a tray and sat down to join us. Mrs. Rocke handed me coffee in a cup and then dropped her bombshell.

"The reason I've asked you here, Miss Cross, is to thank you for the work you were doing for my daughter, and to request that you continue to search for Perry Alms."

She had to be joking. "Mrs. Rocke, I don't know the real reason why Bry wanted me to look for this man, but it's out of my hands now anyway; the police will take over this investigation."

We both waited while behind her a grandfather

clock chimed eleven. Then she said, "I have explained to the police why my daughter employed you, and I don't think they will investigate the matter any further. What you might not have been told last night is that my daughter had received a number of threats recently, and had been to the police about them. Inspector Vann says the killer was evidently a professional, very probably someone brought over from the Continent. There seems little doubt that he is out of the country already."

The carpet beneath my feet was patterned with red and blue birds. Who? I studied the carpet. "Who would want to kill Bry, Mrs. Rocke?"

Across the palm of her right hand she held what must be a rosary. "Rival gambling interests. Bryton did not, of course, tell the police that she was under threat because she was running an illegal casino, but it is likely they had their suspicions. In the past month she'd had her tires slashed, and then a man rang and threatened to bomb the club. Bryton didn't, however, believe she was personally in any real danger. She was wrong."

The wooden beads were polished from use. For a religious woman Mrs. Rocke didn't seem unduly flustered by her daughter's sideline.

Her eyes followed mine. "I tried not to interfere in my daughter's life. I learned long ago that such interference can lead to even greater calamities."

She didn't expand further so I came back to what interested me most, my part in all this. "Why was she looking for Perry Alms? She told me he'd stolen a vase from her but . . ."

The voice that cut in was faintly exasperated. "It is, was, so like Bryton to complicate matters

130

unnecessarily. She didn't want to tell you the real reason because she felt it would have been a betrayal of Charlie Heatton. There were other men in my daughter's life, after Charlie's death, but it was always Charlie who mattered."

Other men, and women, I said to myself. I was pretty sure Bry had played both sides of the tracks.

"I assume Bryton told you about the nightclub they owned in London?"

"Uh-huh." To the left of the clock was an aspidistra, which I found I could barely look at.

"When Bryton heard she had only a short time to live she decided there were certain things she wanted to put in order, and one of the things she had been worried about, for a very long time, was that Perry Alms had not been treated fairly by Charlie. To put it bluntly, Charlie had cheated him. Perry should have had a cut in the first B-Rocke's, but nothing had been put in writing and it became obvious that Charlie had no intention of honoring his side of the agreement. Bryton wasn't happy about this, but she gave in to Charlie on everything. Realizing he'd been cheated out of a great deal of money, Perry walked out. Bryton wished to repay him."

She looked toward the window as if she were searching for someone. "I am hoping that you will find this man, and that I will be able to make good the damage that was done, on my daughter's behalf." Her hands fumbled with a cup and saucer and Joseph discreetly moved forward to assist. "It is very hard to watch your child suffer and not to be able to do anything about it. There was nothing I could do to save my daughter from cancer, but I can do this small thing in her memory. Will you continue in my employ, Miss Cross?"

I said I would. I could hardly say anything else. Mrs. Rocke insisted that money was no object and I was ready to believe her. When I explained that I'd been thinking about a computer search, but had planned to leave this to last because of the cost, she was adamant that I get it done as soon as possible. I promised I'd contact her regularly and she walked me to the front door. As we shook hands I couldn't help thinking that although Bry physically resembled her mother, Mrs. Rocke's self-possession reminded me more of Louise. But not once had Louise been mentioned. It was almost as if with Bry's death Iris Rocke had lost her only child.

PART THREE

CHAPTER TWELVE

By Monday morning the weariness had gone but the numbness was still there. I was in my office and Stephanie was looking at me, wide-eyed. "Wow!" she was saying, "think what would have happened if you hadn't stopped to buy those boots. Boy, were you lucky."

"I'll say." Anchee was sitting on the corner of my desk. "If it weren't for a pair of green wellies I would have been burning paper money in a saucer so you'd have something to spend over on the other side. And then I would have had to light a stick of incense on your desk every morning, to make sure your spirit vacated the premises."

Stephanie's nose wrinkled. "I hate incense, it gives me a sore throat."

"Ghosts don't like it much either." Anchee slid her feet to the floor. "Which must be why it works."

After they'd gone I looked around my office again. A ghost — that explained things. Such as why everything was slightly askew: the shelves, the filing cabinet, the Georgia O'Keeffe print that had suddenly developed a tilt to the right. A ghost: you push the red leather door open and "Kapow!"

"Tor?" Diane hovered in the doorway.

"*C'est moi.*"

"Are you sure you're okay?"

Shot at point blank range. "Of course, I mean I'm still a bit shaky, but that's only to be expected."

She ran a thoughtful finger across a freckled cheekbone. "I don't think you should feel obliged to go on with this case. It would be entirely understandable if you didn't want to."

"I'm fine Diane, really." A nerve under my right eye jumped.

"You don't look fine, you're very pale."

"Loss of blood; it's my period."

Her finger, perched atop the bridge of her nose, looked unconvinced. "Well, if you're sure."

The telephone burred and I grabbed for it, taking the opportunity to wave good-bye to Diane at the same time. "Hello?"

"Hello to you, Ms. Cross."

It wasn't April.

"Hi, Jan. What have you been up to?"

"What have I been up to? Well, I spent yesterday reading the Sunday papers."

"Me too. Amazing, isn't it, how low sterling is against the deutschmark?" Since the weekend the walls, and the carpet, had taken on a distinctly orange tinge, jaundiced rather than peachy.

"I didn't make it to the financial section, I was too busy reading about one Ms. Rocke, a Brighton nightclub owner found murdered on Friday afternoon."

"Did you see what *The Observer* had to say about her? How in the Sixties her London nightclub was well-known for bringing together fashionable socialites with East London wideboys? I thought that was interesting, although they got her age wrong, they said she was fifty-six but I know her younger sister is only forty-two and Bry couldn't have been that much older."

"You're wittering. Look, I thought you said there wasn't a story in all this?"

Tell me a story. I attempted to pull myself together. "What I've been working on has nothing to do with the murder. Although I did find her body, of course."

"You what? Hold on, let me get my pen . . ."

"As well as almost stumbling over the murderer . . ."

"Hold on!"

Well, at least I could still please someone.

A quarter of an hour later Jan was sounding mollified to the point of good-humored and I slipped in a last request that she ask around for any information about one Charlie Heatton. She promised she would and left me free to stare out the window at my section of brick wall.

Yes, no, yes, no . . . my eyes moved across rows of bricks. The yes, no, question that required answering was whether or not I should ring April when I got home. Another, more complex, question was to do with how long a "cooling-off period" was supposed to last.

We'd last seen each other on Saturday afternoon, after I'd got back from Brighton. I'd gone straight to Battersea from the station, and we'd had a major row. Exactly how major I wasn't sure.

"Coffee?" Framed by her black hair and sweater Anchee's face was an oval of lemon. What would she have worn for my funeral, I wondered, black or white?

"Would you really have burned money on my behalf?"

The oval nodded. "Not real money, fake money."

"And the incense?"

"Every day for a month. It's very bad luck for a business to be haunted by an employee. By rivals it's all right. You want coffee or not?"

"Thanks, but not. I've got an appointment with Melanie for a computer search. Why is it all right to be haunted by rivals?"

"Don't ask me, Tor, I don't make up the rules."

Who does? I asked myself as I put on my coat and left the office. Who is it who makes up all the damn, shitty rules?

To get an on-line search done you usually need

to give at least a couple of days' notice, but I'd rung Melanie before nine this morning and she'd just had a cancellation. Melanie runs her business from two small rooms on the third floor of a building off the Strand, a couple of minutes from Charing Cross Station. You can see a corner of the cross itself from one of her windows and I squinted out at it as she sat down at the keyboard. The original cross had been erected in memory of Eleanor of Castile by her husband Edward I in 1290. I knew that because Gareth had told me about it after one of his history lessons. Edward, Hammer of the Scots; Gareth had jumped on and off the sofa, wielding an imaginary club.

"You feeling lucky today, Tor?"

Not remotely. I gave an encouraging grunt, however, turning to watch as the screen filled with incomprehensible data. Melanie had access to several hundred data bases and if Perry Alms had accumulated bad debts, or shares in any off-shore companies, there was a reasonable chance she'd be able to trace him. A lot of the work people like me do by foot and phone, people like Melanie can do from an ergonomically-correct stool, but it does cost: the lady and her Apricot command a cool one hundred pounds an hour. And there's always the possibility that a four-hour search will turn up nothing at all. This itself can either mean a great deal, or nothing at all. In the case of Perry Alms it might mean that he'd taken serious steps to disappear, serious to the extent of changing his name, or even leaving the country; or it might mean nothing more than that he always paid his bills on time and didn't dabble offshore.

After half an hour spent watching Melanie's fingers whiz across the keyboard I left her to it and returned by taxi to the agency.

Back at my desk I leafed through the blue notebook to the list I'd drawn up. 1) Computer check. Picking up a red pen I awarded that a tick. 2) Ring Beverley, the sister of the woman I'd spoken to in Balham, and ask if she knows the whereabouts of Bridget, youngest daughter of Flo Litton. 3) Ring Bridget Litton in order to trace Flo Litton.

I dialed Beverley's number. No answer. File cards, that's what Alicia always suggested at moments like this; write your notes down on file cards and then shuffle them, to see what comes up. The problem was that if numbers one and two drew complete blanks I'd have nothing left to shuffle, not unless I added a number four. I'd thought about a possible four last night, but hadn't included it. Now, with nothing else immediately on the horizon, I did.

Number four warranted just two words, and those two words were a name: Charlie Heatton.

If Melanie came up with any concrete information about Perry I'd be able to cross Charlie off my list. But if she didn't, well . . . What if Charlie hadn't merely cheated Perry? What if he'd got rid of him altogether?

I helped Anchee with some paperwork, made a short trip to the sandwich shop on the corner in order to purchase a date and cream-cheese roll, then tried ringing Beverley again.

She actually answered. "Hello. How can I help you?"

Of course she had Bridget Litton's number, although she was no longer Litton, she'd married

Bernie Smyle a good fifteen years back. She and Bridget didn't communicate often, what with jobs and kids, but their friendship went back a long, long way. Would I tell Bridget hi, and say Bev would be getting in touch?

I replaced the receiver and the phone rang straight back at me. "Tor, this is Melanie." Her tone was pure apology. "I'm sorry, but I've drawn a complete blank."

Four hundred quid didn't buy a great deal these days. "Not a smerrick, eh?"

"Zilch. Are you sure Perry Alms still lives in England?"

I wasn't even sure he was still alive, but that was number four on my list and I had number three to go yet. I breathed deep and dialed the number Beverley had given me for Bridget Smyle, née Litton. After all, Beverley had been home, maybe Bridget was too. She was.

"Good heavens!" she exclaimed, "you've been doing some detective work, to track me all the way from Balham."

She didn't know the half of it. "I have indeed, although it's actually your mother I need to talk to, Mrs. Smyle. She worked in a Mayfair nightclub called B-Rocke's over twenty years ago and I'm hoping to trace someone she knew there."

"Oh, you've been trying to find Mum. I see. I'm sorry to disappoint you Miss Cross, but Mum died a few months back. She'd been in a nursing home since having a stroke, and then passed away in her sleep the night before her eightieth birthday."

So much for number three. Which was virtually the same as saying so much for this case.

"I'm sorry to hear that." This sounded somewhat lame so I added, "It doesn't seem fair she didn't make it to eighty."

"To be quite honest it was a blessing, she'd been very poorly for some time and I hated to see her suffer. It's funny to be reminded about her job at B-Rocke's though, because me and my sister were saying just recently how great it had been when she had that job. She used to bring stuff home, you know, balloons from a party, that sort of thing. And there'd quite often be packets of peanuts and crisps. But then the manager quit and she left soon after, she said it wasn't the same without him."

It is always, but always, worth a try. "Well it's funny you should mention the manager because he's the person I'm looking for. His name was Perry Alms; your mother didn't ever tell you where he went after leaving the club did she? I've been told that she was quite friendly with him and they seemed to know each other from outside work."

"She might very well have told me, but I don't remember. What I do know for sure though is that Mum got all her work through the church. It might sound unlikely but there must have been some link between the nightclub and the church or she wouldn't have worked there."

The nightclub and the church. "Can you remember which church she went to twenty-five years ago?"

"Can I? Miss Cross, up until three years ago my mother went to the church she'd been to since she was born, St. Benet's Roman Catholic Church in Shepherd's Bush. She used to take us there from Balham every Sunday morning." The laugh that came with this was good-natured. "Oh how my sister and I hated that journey."

I thanked her, profusely, then sat back at my desk. The only thing he knew for sure about Perry, Paul Brown had said, was that he believed in God. I just hoped that, a quarter of a century later, Perry Alms was still a believer.

I arrived home to find a cheerful postcard from my Great-Aunt Rosemary, who was visiting friends in San Francisco. Hers was the only message, however; there was nothing, cheerful or otherwise, from my estranged lover, so I found myself running a bath and replaying our last conversation in my mind. The bit that got to me most was when she accused me of trying to emulate my father. "What is it that you expect to get out of this?" she'd demanded. "No one's going to give you a fucking medal, Victoria." She had been curled in the green wicker chair in the corner of her bedroom. The scarf I'd given her was flung over the back of the chair and from it a yellow parrot fixed me with a quizzical eye.

I reached for the strawberry face glop. Back in Oxford I'd been the one who'd made lots of noise so that our potential attackers would flee over the garden wall, while April had been all for tackling them. When I'd pointed this out her reply was that she wasn't saying I was brave but lethally curious.

"Your curiosity has to be satisfied, no matter what. You came close to being killed yesterday, yet you're apparently quite willing to continue to put

143

yourself at risk. Not only is this crazy, it's also unfair to me."

How much of this, I asked myself now, had to do with the difference between a job and a career? Could it be that, deep down, she found my being a private detective, a gumshoe, embarrassing?

"Victoria," she'd said, "are you going to insist on this? Because I'm not sure I can cope if you do."

The weight of this last sentence had dropped like a pebble between us, rolling across a bare wooden floor. I watched this pebble on its journey and knew I could stop it with a phrase. But I also knew that if I said, "You win," there'd be no going back.

"I'm not sure I can cope." Not three words — I love you — but six. Another voice came into my mind, "Oh no, I don't think I could cope with that." This voice was male: Alan, a jovial ex-policeman I'd worked with on a couple of occasions. It was early in the morning and we were sitting in his new Volvo, watching an office block. I'd asked how different private investigation was from being in the force and he'd got onto the topic of working with women. "I reckon it's a good job for a woman, this," he'd said. "Bit of excitement, better than being stuck in some office all day. But I wouldn't want my wife doing it, oh no, I don't think I could cope with that."

The first thing I did after getting into the office the next morning was ring Iris Rocke and tell her that the computer search had been less than a success. When I told her how much it had cost I wasn't surprised when she said it was no problem. What did surprise me was her response when I said I thought Perry Alms was, or at least had been, a Catholic. There was a gasp from her end of the phone and for a moment I thought she'd fainted.

"Mrs. Rocke, are you all right?"

"Yes, yes, of course. It's just that this is such good news."

I could see that it might count as a minor coincidence, but why good news? "Why is it good news, Mrs. Rocke?"

She didn't answer immediately, but then replied, with some dignity, "Because it means that even though he was betrayed by man, he had God, Miss Cross."

My next duty was to contact God's representative at St. Benet's. I'd tried ringing the church after my conversation with Bridget Smyle but there'd been no answer. This morning there was still no reply. I wandered through the office to Diane. She had her feet up on her desk and was reading *The Daily Telegraph*.

"Diane, why are you reading that rag?"

The paper lowered a couple of inches to reveal her chewing on a ballpoint pen. "Because it has the best crossword."

"Oh. Di, remember when you had to ring around various churches, warning them there was a con man on the loose?"

"Hmm."

"Well how did you go about it? It's a Catholic

church I'm interested in, I'm not sure if the number in the phone book is for the church or the priest's residence."

"Third shelf down. No, not there, behind you Tor. That's it, at the far right you'll find *The Catholic Directory*, available from any good bookshop." The newspaper shot up again.

"Right."

"And if that doesn't help, contact the Vicar General's office at Westminster Cathedral."

"Thanks. By the way, what do you *get* out of doing the crossword?" None of the desks were in danger of sliding across the floor today, the calendar on Diane's wall wasn't at an angle. Inside me, however, there was a pebble-sized hole, situated immediately below my ribs.

The paper lowered again. "Doing a crossword is very much like the psychoanalytical process, although it involves playing the role of both analyst and analysand. You have to fill in the gaps by both asking the questions, and supplying the answers. Now what is it that you really want to talk about, Tor?"

The meaning of life, maybe. The possibility of God. Whether or not I needed to start plucking the odd gray hair out of my fringe. Whether or not I could cope with divorce. "Nothing." I backed out the door. "I was just interested, you know. Thanks for the directory."

She shrugged. "Don't mention it."

The Catholic Directory informed me that St. Benet's current incumbent was a Father Ransome, Order of St. Benedict. I dialed his residential number and the phone was answered almost immediately, not by the Father himself but his Irish housekeeper. He'd taken a youth group on a trip, she informed me, and wouldn't be back until tomorrow morning. The minibus was due back at the church at ten-thirty.

Anchee came through and handed me a mug. "It's tea."

"Brilliant, thanks." And then, "What do you want?"

"World peace, an end to pollution. Oh, and high cheekbones."

"You've already got them."

"It's true, we Orientals win out when it comes to cheekbones. Of course we also invented gunpowder and spectacles and writing paper. I believe you lot were grubbing around in the dirt at the time. Speaking of which . . ."

"Uh-huh."

"Blackmail. I've been talking to a prospective client on the phone. He's a businessman who's received an anonymous letter, demanding money, and he's on the verge of frantic. He wants to speak to someone today, and feels he'd be happier discussing his private life with a woman. I told him he'd come to the right place."

"Where is he? Can he make it to the office?"

"His office is close to Paddington, but he'd prefer to meet in a restaurant nearby."

Paddington. I'd driven in this morning; what I could do was slip back to the flat and collect the albums, and then pay Ted a surprise visit on the return trip. He should be back from his hols by now

and it might be an advantage to catch him un-
awares. I could say I'd lost his number and so
hadn't been able to phone first.

"Paddington it is," I said. "My new client can
take me to lunch."

Lunch wasn't a whole heap of fun, but then
neither of us was at our best.

"Of course," I said, and reached for the mineral
water.

"No, I mean it. I want you to understand that
I've never done anything like this before, never been
unfaithful to Miriam. But we've been together twenty
years, and I wanted, oh I don't know, a small
adventure." Taking off his glasses he wiped a
handkerchief across his eyes.

Adventure, well he'd got that. "Do you have the
letter with you?"

"Yes." He fumbled in his wallet. Behind him I
could see the waiter approaching with my chocolate
mousse. Glen hadn't wanted pudding, and hadn't
been able to finish his steak either. I'd noticed
before that the threat of blackmail often worked
wonders for a client's waistline. My own problems
made me want to eat.

"Here." He passed the letter over reluctantly.

It wasn't the worst example of the genre I'd seen
but it was still pretty horrid. As I watched him
tugging at his collar I had a sudden memory of
April, the night we'd met. I hadn't known what was
wrong at the time but had been aware of tension

playing her like a wire. April. My right eye was twitching ominously.

I said, "I know that letters like this are frightening, but there are things we can do. For a start, you must keep each one."

"Dear God," he groaned. "Do you mean there will be others?"

Adventure doesn't come cheap, Glen. "Well it's possible. If there are, keep them, along with the envelopes they come in. And don't handle them too much. We could also do with a sample of your ex-girlfriend's handwriting. Do you have anything she wrote?"

"Look, she was never my girlfriend, it just happened a couple of times, it wasn't anything serious. Miriam's not very well at the moment, she finds it difficult to sleep and we're having problems with our eldest girl . . ."

While he got things off his chest I consoled myself with the chocolate mousse.

Crosswords. You ask yourself the questions and then fill in the answers. Did I love April? I asked myself this at the point where the traffic from Bishop's Bridge Road merged into Westbourne Grove. Yes. Did I want our relationship to end? No. Westbourne Grove became Pembridge Road and then a right turn brought me into Notting Hill Gate. Gray clouds gathered overhead, and as I parked down the road from Ted's the sky began to spit. Next question: how long does a cooling-off period last? I don't know. That's three words, nine letters. Is there a God? Same answer. Life after divorce?

At the top of the stairs I shook out my umbrella, wondering if the friendly neighbor would make an appearance again today. He didn't. There was no response to my first knock so I tried again.

"Who's there?" A girl's voice.

The fuzz, open up! I put my face close to the door and called back. "I was here last week, I've come to see Ted."

The door opened a couple of inches. "It's you."

"Is Ted in? I've brought his albums back. I lost the phone number or I would have rung."

The gap got wider. As she peered out I could see that today she was in jeans and a black sweater, looking like a regular teenager rather than a born-again hippie. "Why don't you keep them?" she suggested. "I wouldn't fucking give them back."

I liked the sentiment, but was less sure about her face. "Are you all right?"

"Yeah." She stepped out into the hall. "Is it raining or something?"

I noted with relief that the bruised look was due to a combination of smudged mascara and eyeliner. "It started just as I got here."

"Fuck. I've got all this stuff."

Looking over her shoulder I saw a suitcase and some plastic bags. "Where are you off to?"

"To the Tube, a friend's got me a room at Earl's Court. But don't tell *him* that will you?"

"I certainly won't."

"He's a jerk and I'm leaving. He's taken up with this slag, Bronwyn, and now she's here all the time and he treats me more like shit than ever. She's older than me, nineteen, but he likes her because she does stuff that I won't." Her look was defiant. "Does that surprise you, there's stuff I won't do?"

I shook my head. "It doesn't surprise me at all, Cho." Her face brightened; remembering her name was a huge compliment. "How about I give you a lift to the Tube?"

"Would you?"

"No problem. I'll come back and see Ted some other time."

The suitcase was already in her hand. "Like I said, don't bother, he only gave them to you to make sure you would come back."

"Can I take that?" A large blue hat box had made an appearance. "Why did he want to see me again?"

She slammed the door behind her. "Because there was this bloke who planned to follow you. Ted tried to ring him while you were here, but the bloke was away and so Ted had to make sure you'd come back again. He's a right cunning bastard."

"Cho, how about I drive you all the way to Earl's Court, and you tell me about it. Deal?"

"Too right!"

The rain was steady now and the traffic was moving warily.

"So who was it who wanted me followed?" I glanced at her. "Is your seat belt on?"

She fumbled with the buckle. "This guy who turned up last summer. He was asking questions about the same man."

"You mean Perry Alms?"

"Whoever, the same one you were asking about."

"And did Ted tell him anything?"

"I think so, but I don't know what it was. I got ordered out to the kitchen to make coffee. He always sends me out to make coffee. You know what?" She drew her right foot up under her.

"What's that?"

"I spit in it. I saw this movie where a black chick did it to some old fart. It was great!"

"I know the movie you mean."

"But I didn't spit in the coffee I made you, I only do it to Ted."

"In your position I'd do the same. What was this man like? How old was he?"

She reflected. "Pretty old, over forty; but not as old as Ted. He looked like he was half dago, you know, Italian or Greek, and he was wearing a dark blue suit so I thought he might have been a businessman. But he was okay. He was quiet like, and polite. I could tell he didn't like the way Ted treated me. He didn't like Ted either but of course Ted-the-Fucking-Man didn't notice that."

"What did he say to Ted?"

"Well he was asking about this bloke, and then he said to Ted that if anyone else ever came asking the same questions Ted wasn't to tell them anything.

He said Ted should make sure the person came back so he could follow them. He gave him some money, I know that much."

"Did he explain any of this?" A double-decker bus pulled out in front and I quickly felt for the brake.

"No. But I don't think he was planning to do anything bad. I think he was trying to protect this bloke, Perry. I know I said he was a dago but I don't think he was going to knife anyone." Her voice was confidential. "I get feelings about people, if they're okay or not. I knew you were okay from the start."

The bus slowed down and so did I. Maybe her information meant Perry Alms was alive after all. But who else was looking for him, and why?

"And I know what you're thinking but I knew Ted was an arsehole, it's just I didn't have a choice right then. It was either living with him or sucking off geezers in doorways. You'd have chosen Ted too."

She was right, I would.

Back at the office I called an emergency conference. For once everyone was in.

"What do you think?" I asked.

Stephanie threw a paper plane into her bin. "I think you should let the police know. You said you liked the one in charge. See what he says first."

"I agree," said Anchee, "we can't afford for you to get your throat cut, Tor, we're short-staffed as it is."

"What about the girl?" Diane was sitting on the

arm of Steph's chair. "Do you feel she's probably right about this man, and he's not a physical threat?"

Stephanie snorted. "You can't take risks because a druggie teenager didn't pick up any bad vibes."

My instincts were that Cho's instincts were right, but I'd check with Inspector Vann all the same. "If I go ahead with this I'll need two cars."

"Not tonight." Stephanie turned her hands into binoculars. "Tonight I'm watching a Mr. Ingham's bedroom window on behalf of Mrs. Ingham, who's away visiting her aunt in the country. But I'm free tomorrow night, or Friday."

I went off to ring police headquarters in Brighton.

The Inspector hesitated, no doubt twirling his bow tie. "I'm not at liberty to tell you exactly what direction our investigations are taking of course —"

I cut in. "But I've got a good idea from talking to Mrs. Rocke. Bry's murder seems to be linked to her gambling activities, it doesn't have anything to do with Perry Alms. All the same, it is odd that someone is willing to follow anyone making enquiries."

"Quite. You're wise to be cautious." There was a brief silence. "I take it that you have colleagues you can rely on? And that you've done this sort of thing before?"

"Yes on both counts." I made my voice as professional as possible. "We would hope to get a photo of the man. If we're successful in following him back to where he's living we might even be able to come up with a name. I was thinking I'd send a copy of the photo to you, in case you recognize him."

"Do that. And, Miss Cross, take care."

At nine that night I poured myself a second brandy and rang April. Ruth, the babysitter, answered and I put the phone down without saying anything.

CHAPTER THIRTEEN

"Here, run your finger along the shaft. Do you feel that? Throbbing with power that is. What you're holding there, Tor, is the power of the elements themselves."

I was in Frankie and Hughie Deloraine's kitchen, my novice fingers wrapped around a bleached piece of driftwood.

"Now feel this, it hasn't been in the water that long, feel the texture. Different isn't it?"

"Very." Their enthusiasm was infectious. I pointed the rougher piece at the kitchen wall in front of me, a mosaic of wood, shells, water-worn glass. "Does anybody know about you? Anybody in the art world that is?"

"My dear!" Frankie clicked his tongue. "We've been on breakfast television."

"That's right," his twin said nodding. "Outsider Art, that's what we are. We could be another Gilbert and George, if the art establishment wasn't so hidebound. More tea, and what about a biscuit?"

I accepted a chocolate bourbon, and Frankie leaned forward on his elbows. "So Father Ransome's back from his latest jaunt?"

Frankie was the resident Roman Catholic; Hughie had announced he was an atheist. "That's the advantage in not being identical," he'd explained. "I got the brains. How anyone can believe in all that hogwash is beyond me." As soon as Frankie and I began talking about the priest, Hughie went through to the next room to sort through a bucket of dry seaweed.

"Don't mind him." Frankie winked. "I converted thirty years ago and I'm used to it. Now what was our good priest up to when you called?"

"He was helping a bunch of teenagers unload enormous backpacks out of a minibus." Actually he hadn't been helping anybody, he'd been doing it all himself. Father Ransome gave a whole new meaning to the concept of muscular Christianity.

"He's terribly Outward Bound," Frankie confided. "In the old days the entire Sunday School sat there like mushrooms singing 'Telephone to Jesus.' These days they go white-water rafting. Not everyone approves of course. Now, what did he say about me?"

Just for starters he'd said Frankie was an amiable eccentric who enjoyed a good gossip. "He said if anyone could remember a member of the congregation who used to attend over twenty years ago it would be you."

"And he'd be right. Hughie might have got the brains but I got the memory. Who is it you're looking for?"

"Perry Alms," I said. "Do you remember him?"

"Why darling, of course I remember him. He was a regular attender who suddenly stopped attending. Poor old Father Doyle was quite distressed. I hadn't seen Perry Alms for years and years, and then I did see him again and now you're here looking for him. Isn't that strange?"

One, two, three; I'm counting slowly. "When was it you saw him, Frankie? Was it long ago?"

He sipped his tea. "Hughie always makes it too strong. No it wasn't long at all, in fact it was about a month ago, on the twenty-sixth of December, to be precise."

If Frankie was right Perry Alms wasn't at the bottom of the Thames but, on Boxing Day at least, had been in the Brompton Oratory for a mass celebrating St. Stephen.

"I've absolutely no doubt it was him, he'd hardly changed. I waved but he didn't see me and by the time I'd made it to the porch he was gone. I did think about going to the Oratory again but I must admit I find the place off-putting: a stone's throw from Harrods, with much the same clientele. Perry used to attend St. Benet's every Sunday, but I do remember him saying that he liked to go to the Brompton Road for feast days. If you find him, say hello from me won't you? He was always very kind about the shells."

"Seaweed?" Anchee frowned.

"Dried," I said. Despite the fact that everything was set up for tonight's visit to Ted-the-Man, and I had what appeared to be a definite lead to Perry Alms, my right temple was throbbing and I was waiting for two dispirin to dissolve in a glass of water. Who was it who'd said there were times when they wanted to "dissolve in a glass, like a dispirin"?

"And this seaweed was on the wall?"

I nodded, and pain darted from my temple into my right eye. "Along with shells and bits of wood. What's wrong with seaweed, anyway? You eat the stuff." Whenever we went Chinese in Soho, Anchee could be counted on to winkle out shrimp brains with the end of her chopstick. I mean, how authentic could you get?

"Woops Tor, your ethnocentricity is showing. It's that other lot, the Japanese, who are big on seaweed. But to get back to the point, you eat cabbage but you haven't wallpapered your living room with it. Or you hadn't the last time I visited. And speaking of paper, I need some hours, soon, or next month's rent won't be getting paid."

"Quit worrying, I'll do it now." Carrying the glass

back to my office, I remembered who'd made the
comment about dissolving like a dispirin — Princess
Di. Which just goes to show there's always someone
whose life is even grottier than your own.

CHAPTER FOURTEEN

Paola brought over another basket of garlic bread. "You are still waiting for Stephanie, si?"

Steph was due to meet us at six. I'd told Ted I'd be at his place by eight, or shortly after. "Si. She should be here soon, Paola." *Here* wasn't Gino's but Carlo's, a pizzeria owned by Paola and Carlo, her half-brother. Carlo's was further away from the agency but had in its favor the fact that it was situated halfway down a brightly-lit arcade, with a pub on the corner and a coffee shop opposite.

Situation was all-important if our plans for this evening were going to work.

"Thanks Paola." Reaching for more bread, Diane continued, "Julia Kristeva isn't actually French. She's lived in France for donkey's years, but originally hailed from Bulgaria."

"But the others, they're French, aren't they?"

"Hélène Cixous and Luce Irigaray are both French." I was being given an introductory lecture on psychoanalytic feminist theory. "Anyway, as I was saying, where some of this stuff radically challenges the Freudian model is in the suggestion that we choose our gender role at an early age, by following the pattern of either our mother or father."

I was tempted to ask what happened if you had only one parent, or even no parents at all, but things were already complicated enough. "And gender doesn't depend on biological sex, is that right?" I've always been good at playing the nerdy bookworm.

"Precisely. Now picture a circle. At the center you have what's known as the symbolic, that's the area of language, of law and order, and patriarchy. Around the edges of the circle you have a marginal area, where language, law and order, break down. The circumference is also the area of the subversive, the feminine. That's why the feminine is always threatening you see; it's supposed to act as a buffer against the outer chaos, but the problem is that it's also in close proximity to that chaos. The good mother can do an about-turn and suddenly become the evil queen, allowing destruction into the world. Hence, madonnas and whores. Are you with me?"

"I think so." My orange juice had left a

subversive ring on the green-checked table cloth. Dangerous wet patches were soaking toward the center.

"Right. But where you position yourself in terms of gender doesn't have anything to do with your biological sex, or with your sexuality. Take Margaret Thatcher as an example. Biologically female; heterosexual; but positioned right at the center of the circle, in a masculine gender position. You see?" She seemed inordinately pleased with this example.

"Oh yes." Well, sort of. Over on the other side of the room a party waited while Paola pulled two tables together. One of the waiting men reached up to a light fixture and tugged at a piece of green and gold tinsel left over from Christmas, and carefully draped it over the heads of two of his male companions.

"Boy, am I hungry." Stephanie dumped her carpet bag on the floor and gave a wolfish grin. "Are you lusting after those hunks over there, Tor? If so we can double-date."

Whereabouts in the circle was Stephanie? If it came to that, where was I? "Any time you want, Steph, I know a lady called Fran who'd think you were awfully cute. By the way, have you got the mobile phones?"

"Check, in the bag. And the alarm. And the headgear." She flung her shawl over the back of a chair. "Is your car out the back, Di? And did you bring the camera?"

Diane nodded and handed over her car keys. "Ladies," she said, "let's eat."

At a quarter to seven, after we'd talked things

163

over with Carlo and Paola again, it was time to move. "Are we all clear about what's happening?" I asked.

"Yep." Steph handed Diane one of the phones. "I'll ring you as soon as we leave Notting Hill. Now I'm going to the loo. I'll meet you out in Bill's taxi, Tor."

"I need to powder my nose too. Will you be okay waiting, Di?"

She reached into her bag for a paperback. "The latest Patricia Highsmith," she said. "I'm here for the rest of the evening."

Bill was used to us as passengers by now and he happily stopped his taxi to let Steph off first, at the corner of Ladbroke Grove and Elgin Crescent. Earlier in the day she'd parked her car just down the road from Ted's flat. "You're sure you won't find you've been wheel-clamped?" I asked.

"Sure I'm sure, you don't need a permit around here. It'll take me five minutes to walk there."

"Fine. We'll arrive at eight on the dot."

"And Tor, if you're not happy about the way things are going up there you just hit that alarm. Ted won't hear anything but I'll have the receiver on and I'll be up those stairs before you can say Wonder Woman."

"Don't forget I'm here too," Bill called back over his shoulder. "I know you ladies can handle yourselves but a hard right to the guts has its place. Anybody touches either of you and I'll be more than happy to oblige."

164

Ten minutes later we drew up outside the flat. From the corner of my eye I'd seen Steph sitting in her car but I'd been careful not to turn my head. I was also careful not to look for occupants in any of the cars parked in Ted's street.

"You right, pet?" Bill asked softly.

"Yes." I got out and spoke clearly through the window. "I won't be long, you don't mind waiting, do you?"

"No," Bill bellowed back. "You take as long as you like, Miss. There isn't anywhere to park but I'll keep the engine idling." He'd once told me he'd had aspirations to be an actor, which no doubt explained why he enjoyed these jaunts with us.

There was no patchouli tonight, but Ted answered on my first knock. "Why hello there!" he was in danger of gushing. "Please do come in."

Where Cho had attempted a Nineties version of a Sixties hippie chick, Bronwyn was a mutant Goth. Her black dress was festooned with plastic skull brooches.

Ted gloated over his latest protege. "She's obsessed with vampires. Aren't you, Bronwyn?"

Bronwyn glowered at me. She had the pallor down pat, all she lacked were the fangs.

Smiling politely I held out the plastic carrier bag. "Thank you for the albums, they were really interesting. Have you come across the letter, Ted?" I attempted to look, and sound, hopeful. The way I envisaged it, Ted would say that he was very sorry but he hadn't, and I'd then be able to make good my escape and get on with the main events of the evening. Ted, however, had envisaged things differently.

"It took me a couple of days but I did find something. I'll go get it."

"That's great!" What the fuck was he up to? Bronwyn shot me a vitriolic look from the sofa.

"Here." Ted was back in an instant. "We had a deal, remember? Fifty quid if I helped you locate Perry. Well I've lost the letter he wrote me but I found the envelope. There's Perry's name and address on the back." He waved an envelope in front of me and gave a yellow smile.

Whom did he think he was dealing with? Look here, sunshine, I invented this one. "That's really wonderful," I simpered. "But how do I know he'll still be there? You tell me the address, Ted, and if I find him I'll pay you the fifty pounds. Promise."

He managed not to stamp his feet, but only just. "Now that's not very fair is it? If you find him you'll inherit all that money and I'll never hear from you again."

I opened my eyes wide. "But I brought your albums back didn't I? You can trust me, Ted."

"Ask Bronwyn." His voice broke into a growl. "Ted-the-Man doesn't trust no one. Now either you hand over fifty pounds, like you promised, or you get out of here."

As his hopes of squeezing an extra fifty out of me were dwindling, so too was his nice-guy routine. I shrugged with haughty innocence. "Somebody else has said he can help me, and I didn't offer him any money at all. I'm sorry you don't trust me but I'm not going to pay for something that might be useless. I'd better be going." An exit right was called for here, but Ted was suddenly between me and the door.

"Fuck you, you cheap bitch. Who do you think you are, coming here and trying to rip me off?"

"I'm leaving," I said. Despite the fact that I wasn't.

"Suck my dick, you're leaving." He leaned against the door and gestured for Bronwyn to join him. "That's a good idea, don't you think Bron? If Miss Tightarse here wants to leave without paying what she owes, she can suck my dick."

I slipped my left hand into my pocket and found the alarm. We weren't at the emergency stage yet, although it had to be said that things had taken a decidedly unpleasant turn.

Ted's laugh was unpleasant too. "But you wouldn't like that, would you? You're not interested in cock are you, you dykey bitch?" His voice was malicious over the top of Bronwyn's head. "You should have heard her getting the hots for that slag, Cho. Ooh Cho," he put on a high voice, "what lovely eyes you have Cho, they match your dress. Ooh Cho, I'd like to shove my fat tongue right up your fat cunt. Is that what you'd like to do with Bronwyn here?" He pushed her slightly forward. "Show her your tits, Bron. I'm going to enjoy watching this bitch creaming herself." Bronwyn obediently began unbuttoning the front of her dress and Ted's hands moved down to his fly.

As I felt the weight of the alarm in my hand, a lesson Gareth had learned in a stranger-danger session popped into my mind: Walk, Don't Run. And Don't Look Back. I stepped forward as confidently as I could and yanked firmly at the door handle. The door didn't budge, and neither did Ted. I pulled at the handle again and he suddenly stepped forward so that the door shot open, slamming me across the right cheek.

"Lesbo slag!" Bronwyn screamed from the top of the stairs. I didn't run down, I walked. And I didn't look back.

"Did the bastard hit you?" Bill was ready to jump out of his cab.

I gingerly touched my cheek where a bump was forming already. "No, I just wasn't watching where I was going. Let's go." The creep wasn't worth the bother.

We took a long route so that Steph would have time to spot whoever was following us and still be able to arrive first and swap over into Diane's car.

Bill kept a check on his rear mirror. "That's it," he said. "A black Honda. There are two blokes." There would be, one to do the driving and the other to jump out and follow on foot if need be. Cho's man in the blue suit knew what he was about. "Can't see the registration from here."

"Don't worry, Steph will get that."

"You sure you don't want me to hang around and trail him for you?"

"He might recognize you, Bill."

"That's true," he said, nodding. "I'll drop you at the arcade entrance then." His voice brightened. "Till tomorrow night then?"

"You'll be able to do all the trailing you want to then."

"I'll enjoy that. It's something I'm good at, if I do say so myself."

"I know. That's why I asked."

I got out and paid him through the window,

making sure that our friends had enough time to see where I was going. Then I walked quickly through the arcade until I came to Carlo's. A birthday was being celebrated at a long table at the front and as I walked through the door Diane came forward, holding a camera. "Everybody smile!" she called out. A cheer went up. I walked straight through the restaurant and out into the kitchen.

"Ciao!" Carlo nonchalantly waved from where he and Paola were decorating a cake with pastel candles. Paola nodded in the direction of another door and I stepped out into the back courtyard. The gate was unlocked and outside it Steph was waiting in Diane's car, the motor running.

"Here you go." She handed me the blond wig. Her own hair was concealed under a peasant scarf.

"Why do I always get the wig? You're not the only one who looks good in a scarf." Not that I looked as good as Steph, but there was the principle of the thing.

"Shut it. I've got too much hair to go under a wig. Now put that thing on and let's get going."

We turned left at the corner then left again.

"There," she said, nodding at the black car.

It was almost ten minutes before a man in a long gray coat strode out of the arcade and climbed back in. "He must be well and truly pissed off," she chortled.

I had a sudden flash of Ted's face, distorted with anger. "He certainly must."

Stephanie laughed, her eyes fixed on the car. "Is she in the pub, our man asks himself. No, can't see her here. Maybe she's gone to the loo?"

I joined in. "Maybe she has. But I'd better check that restaurant first. Can I see her in there? No, all I can see in there is a photographer."

"They're moving." Steph left a good twenty-yard gap. "Don't worry Tor, I won't lose them."

Steph didn't lose them, they lost us.

"Shit! I'm sorry Tor." The Honda had jumped a red light and a nightbus was hurtling across our path.

"It's not your fault, I don't want to be squashed either."

"But it means they must have seen me, and I've been so careful."

"Yeah, well they're probably just being careful too. I have the feeling these guys have done this before."

"Stolen license plates?"

"More than likely. Come on Steph, the lights have changed."

Steph apologized all the way back to the agency, where I'd left Lucy. "Forget it," I told her for the umpteenth time. "There wasn't anything you could have done."

"You mean it?"

"I do. I'll see you tomorrow."

I cursed my way back to Hoxton. The lights were on in the flat and as I opened the door I could hear the television as well. Damn, I wasn't exactly in the mood for company. "Denise?" I hung my coat on the hook at the top of the stairs. "I didn't expect..."

"Hi."

It wasn't Denise, it was April.

"April." Oh Jesus, was everything going to be all right, or not?

She'd turned the television off and was standing in the middle of the room. "I've been a complete cow. I'm sorry Victoria, really sorry, but I was so frightened. Do you remember how you felt in Oxford, when I was in danger?" Her face crumpled. "Can you forgive me?"

Given the chance to plan this scene I would have swept her into my arms at this point, kissing away her tears whilst murmuring, magnanimously, that of course I forgave her. As it was, relief replaced apprehension and the result was a wave of nausea that hit me deep in the gut, bringing along with it an image which I'd been keeping at a distance for the past few days. The image was of Bry Rocke, under the table. I'd stared at her, and as I stared blood had soaked across the front of her green dress, a brown trail of vine and leaves slowly spreading across her chest.

"Victoria? Sweetheart, are you okay?"

Clamping my hand across my mouth I dashed to the bathroom and threw up.

CHAPTER FIFTEEN

"Dear God!" Fran stared down at me in horror. "Tor, whatever happened to you?"

"Dreadful isn't it?" I peeked coyly over the top of the menu. "This time the electrolysis went terribly wrong. But don't worry, I'll be able to sue." Fran was one of the few people I'd told about my visit to the beauty clinic to have the veins taken care of.

Fran was fascinated, as I knew she would be. She slid into a chair and stared at my cheek. "Surely electrolysis couldn't do that! Could it?"

"I found out later the beautician was sozzled.

Hey!" I jumped back as she put out a tentative finger. "Don't do that, it's sore."

"I don't believe you."

"It hurts a lot, in fact." Well, it hurt a bit.

"I don't believe that was caused by electrolysis. It looks to me like someone hit you."

I watched as a dreadful thought took shape. That was one of the things I loved about Fran, her transparency. It was also what caused a lot of her problems, of course.

"No, April and I have not been having violent rows, Fran." Just nonviolent ones.

Relief was mixed with a drop of disappointment. "Of course not, I never thought..."

"You did too. As it happens I walked into a door last night. Sort of."

We were trying out Covent Garden's latest salad bar. In the middle of winter I'd actually prefer a pie and chips, but trendy places like this don't run to high carbohydrates.

"Suzanna hasn't rung." Fran picked her way through a bowl of beans and tofu. "So I guess I won't be hearing from her again."

I didn't mention the fact that sweet Sue had phoned to discuss the effect my arches had on her libido. "She wasn't what I'd call viable in the long-term."

A piece of tofu fell from Fran's fork into her glass of Perrier. She didn't appear to notice. "It's because I'm hungry, isn't it?"

"What do you mean?" The tofu was settling into sludge at the bottom of the glass. "By the way you need a new —"

She reached for the glass and took a sip. "I'm

hungry for love, that's why nothing works out. It scares people off."

Her hand as it held the glass could have been the hand of a woman of fifty or sixty. Why is it that our hands go first? "I think it does scare some people. But that's a poor comment on them isn't it?" I'd been terribly needy when I met April, but that hadn't seemed to worry her. I looked out through the window towards the arches of Covent Garden; after lunch I'd go in search of a present, a love-token.

Fran followed my gaze and we watched a toddler in a blue and yellow coat way too big for him run at some pigeons. They shot up then descended a few feet further on. On a pillar in the background an official sign read: *If you like feeding birds, buy yourself a budgie. Please don't feed the pigeons.*

"I can remember a time when old ladies sold plastic cups of birdseed to the tourists at Trafalgar Square," Fran mourned. "I walked across the Square on my way here today and you know what I saw? Rats. Two of them. Can you believe that? I suppose it's not really surprising, the Victorian sewers are about to cave in at any minute. Whole areas of London are due to collapse."

"They were probably mice." A tour leader marched past the window, carrying a rolled red umbrella above his head, trailed by three Japanese tourists. "I watched a documentary on telly which said the Tube's crowded with mice. They live off crumbs, and human hair."

Fran picked up her glass and quizzically peered

into it. "They weren't mice, they were rats. Snuffling round the base of Nelson's Column like they owned him. But let's talk about something more cheerful, Tor. Tell me, how goes the detective business these days? Stumbled over any dead bodies?"

After parting company with Fran I stopped at one of the Covent Garden stalls and chose a small wooden box decorated with a stenciled picture.

"It's a scene from a Russian fairy story." The woman who ran the stall had also decorated the box. "See the princess?" The woman's finger was red with cold. "She's been captured by a wicked magician, but here comes her mother, who's a witch, to save her. The mother finishes up making a deal; her daughter spends six months of the year with her, and six months with the magician. Them's the breaks."

"Persephone and Demeter," I contributed. According to the ancient maps, Hell was at the center of the circle.

"The same." She handed me the box wrapped in lavender tissue paper.

The next row of stalls included a selection of second-hand paperbacks and I half-heartedly picked up an old copy of *The Moosewood Cookbook*. Maybe if I started buying cookbooks an interest in the subject would develop naturally. Next to *Moosewood* was something entitled *The Hungry Monk*. And next to that, a copy of *Brighton Rock*, by Graham Greene. The first date of publication was 1938. Kismet, I told myself. Replacing the cookbooks I forked out one pound and fifty pence for the paperback and headed off to the office.

"You okay there, Tor?" Steph had brought through another sheaf of statements for me to check.

"I'm fine. I'll be finished with these soon. Here are the ones I think you'll find of use." I indicated a small pile.

"Not many." She glared at the pile. "Are the rest all complete dross?"

"None of them would stand up in court."

"Drat it." Catching sight of a long hair caught on her sleeve she picked it off and dropped it on my carpet. "I must say you're looking better"

"You think this suits me then?" I pointed at my bruise.

"Apart from that you look better. I was worried about you at the beginning of the week, you looked like you were coming down with something."

I'd been in danger of a badly broken heart. "I was feeling a bit under the weather."

"Diane did a brilliant job with the photos didn't she?"

"She did. I particularly like the one where he's peering straight in through the window, looking terribly puzzled."

Steph laughed. "Nonplussed. You can see him thinking, where the fuck has that bitch disappeared to?"

"You certainly can. Diane reckons he was over six foot, possibly six-two or six-three. He fits Cho's description all right, olive complexion, maybe part Greek or Italian."

"He did the driving from Notting Hill, and is obviously our main man. Are you sending any of the photos to the police?"

"I've already done it, with a note to the Inspector, asking if he recognizes him. I've also put one in the post to Iris Rocke, in case he's someone she knows."

"So what happens next?"

"Knightsbridge," I said.

"The Harrods sale?"

"The Conversion of St. Paul."

Hyde Park Corner. Ma took us there as children to listen to the speakers. Democracy, she'd explained, means freedom of speech. This is what your father fought for.

I'd found it terribly disappointing, the thought that my hero father had risked his life so that unwashed nutters could stand on vegetable boxes and predict the end of the world, or warn against the danger to society that came from drinking too much tea. When I was an undergraduate, Hyde Park Corner was where you met your friends before joining marches protesting for lesbian and gay rights, or against nuclear weapons. During my stint in the archives the park had disappeared from my world altogether, reappearing, when I joined the agency, as the northern border of Knightsbridge, where every so often I was summoned to hear the personal trials of the very rich. "It isn't easy," they confided in rooms overlooking the Palace Gate, the Albert Memorial, "having money. It turns one into a victim, at the mercy of the unscrupulous." The rooms always smelled of old fur and flowers.

Tonight I emerged out of the Knightsbridge Tube and mentally placed Hyde Park Corner a few streets to the east. With that as the top right corner of my map, I cut diagonally left along Cromwell Road until I came to the Brompton Oratory.

Bill was parked outside. I tapped on his window. "Hi there."

"Hello Tor." We watched a group of glossy young women walk past, wearing identical leather jackets, tight jeans and knee-high boots, the boots with narrow heels and gold buckles at the ankle. "And they reckon the economy's fallen apart." He shook his head. "There's no shortage of loot in this neck of the woods, is there?"

The night felt cold enough for snow. "There isn't. I'm sorry, I should have bought you a hot drink on the way."

"Got a thermos." He patted the seat next to him. "You going in there to say your prayers then are you?" He nodded in the direction of the domed building.

"I'll be praying all right. But a non-believer like me mightn't get results so this could turn out to be a long night during which nothing happens at all. If that's the case I apologize in advance."

He laughed. "Doesn't worry me, pet. I'm getting paid and I've got the crossword to do. You take your time."

When I'd rung the church the duty priest had informed me that for the Conversion of St. Paul there would be special masses tonight at seven-thirty, eight, nine and ten. I desperately hoped that not only would Perry Alms want to celebrate this particular feast, but that he'd also want to do it at a reasonable hour. I climbed the Oratory's shallow steps, crossed my fingers at the top, and stepped for the first time into London's most-celebrated Roman Catholic Church.

Colored marble, statuary; overhead the ceilings were aglow with gold stars in an azure heaven. The air was thick with candle wax and incense. How was it that I'd never been here before? It was amazing. It was completely over the top. It was wonderful. With Mass not due to begin for fifteen minutes or so, I wandered down the central nave, noting the chapels off to each side. In one a woman in a fur coat sat and prayed; in another, the Lady Chapel, a young man lit a candle to join the dozens already burning. Above his head a pale-lipped Mary was swathed in blue and gold, a white-clad baby in her arms.

I decided that the best position to take up would be right at the back of the nave, between the two entrances. I could loiter there while people came in.

Perry had hardly changed, Frankie said. I had the photos of Perry in my pocket, but was pretty sure I could recognize him without them. If I didn't see anyone who looked like Perry I could either stay where I was, or join the congregation.

Perry Alms wasn't one of the fifty-two people who attended the seven-thirty mass. I didn't count everyone as they came in, it was just something to do after they were all seated. There were two main rows of pews, one each side of the nave. In front of the Lady Chapel, however, to the right of where most people were sitting, half a dozen pews stood by themselves and from here I studied my fellow worshippers. Out of the fifty-two, thirty-one were women, which left twenty-one men. Out of the twenty-one, fifteen looked to be forty or over, and I was sure that Perry Alms wasn't one of those fifteen.

There was a queue for communion, "The body of Christ." The priest's voice mixed with the sound of feet shuffling on stone floors, the odd cough from the pews. A white napkin wiped the rim of a silver chalice. "The blood." A young girl turned toward me and smiled with a wet, purple mouth.

"No luck then?" Bill wound down his window when I knocked.

"He wasn't there, I'm sure of that." I hugged myself against the cold.

"Would you like a cuppa? I've got a clean cup."

"I wouldn't say no."

I climbed into the back and he handed over a steaming mug. "And here's some whitener. Sugar?"

"No thanks." I put the mug down on the floor and took off my gloves. "You're not too bored then?"

"My only complaint is that people keep trying to climb in; why don't they ever bother to check whether the sign's on or not? Apart from that I'm happy as Larry. I could never be bored with a crossword. Do you do 'em at all?"

"Never." I waited till the next car's headlights swept past, then hastily spooned whitener into the tea. "I can't understand the fascination. I mean, what do you get out of it?" My fingers stung pleasantly with the heat of the cup.

"I know this'll probably sound pretentious." His voice was mellow in the dark. "But I sometimes think doing the crossword's a bit like that lot in there. You get the feeling you've solved a tiny mystery. That's what it's all supposed to be about, isn't it, solving a mystery?" He swung round. "Told you it sounded pretentious, didn't I?"

I blew noisily on the tea so I didn't have to agree with him.

I found Perry Alms.

To be honest, I don't know whether I really expected I'd find him or not. Sometimes you set out on someone's trail knowing, deep in your guts, that you're not going to locate them. Other times you have this feeling that you will. With Perry I didn't have any strong intuitions, although when he walked into the church it was like seeing someone I knew, and respected. Peregrine, I thought as I watched him cross himself. Peregrine the pilgrim; the good man. His eyes were clear above wide cheekbones and a strong chin. Where, I wondered, have you been for the past twenty-five years? I sat on the pew behind him. His bowed head was brown streaked with gray;

under the turned-up collar of his tweed coat his scarf was blue.

He was always, Frankie had said, kind about the shells.

All that Iris Rocke required was that I locate him; she would make any approaches herself. Bryton's last request. As soon as the Mass finished I scurried out of the church to the taxi.

"Spotted him, have you?"

I checked over my shoulder. "He's coming down now. In the tweed coat. Can you see him?"

"I can."

"If he walks I'll follow, and you try to keep us in sight."

"Looks like he's going for a taxi to me. He's heading straight down here, not toward the pedestrian crossing. You better climb in, Tor, or he'll be hiring me himself."

I hadn't thought of that, Bill would be able to drive him all the way home! "Bill, that's it, let him hire you!"

"Get in woman, it's too late for that; the gentleman's hailed himself a conveyance." Perry's habits hadn't changed then. I wondered where he bought his biscuits these days.

"I'll take a bet." Bill followed the other car as it took another right turn. "Where we're heading is St. John's Wood, or maybe a posh part of Swiss Cottage. Got money has he?"

"I have absolutely no idea. What I do know is that he's going to be better off as a result of this. Someone owes him money from over twenty years ago."

"Some people are born lucky aren't they?" We shot forward. "Sorry about that but I thought we were going to miss the lights. Not that it's a tragedy if I do lose him because I've taken the other bloke's number and he can tell us where he took his fare. I'd sit back and enjoy the trip if I were you."

I did.

Twenty minutes later the first taxi stopped and Bill cruised on past. "There he is. Nice part of town isn't it?"

"Very." What we were cruising past was a row of Victorian town houses.

"Jammy bastard, how do folk do it?"

"He might be the butler." But I didn't believe it.

"Not in a coat like that." We made a U-turn at the end of the road, drove slowly back and pulled up opposite the house. "Most places this big are divided into flats, but not this lot," Bill noted. "Now you've got the street name and the house number, haven't you?"

"I have." The ground floor lights were on. I wondered if anyone else was home. Whom did Perry Alms live with? What work, if any, did he do? I might hear the answers to these questions sometime in the future, or I might not. My part in all this was over. I rested my forearm on the back of Bill's seat. "You know, Watson, I think I can say this case is solved."

"A job well done, eh? Where next Madam?"

"Battersea," I said. "South of the river, and don't spare the horses."

* * * * *

April was in bed. "What's the time?" she mumbled.

"Quarter to eleven. A tiring day?" I nibbled at her left earlobe.

"Mmm. I'm knackered. What have you been doing?"

"I've been to church." I nibbled further down.

"That's nice."

"That I went to church and prayed for us?"

"What you're doing to my neck. You'll have to tell me about church tomorrow, I'm too tired to take it in now. I'm sorry."

So was I; I was far too excited to sleep. I waited till she'd burrowed under the duvet and then I padded through to the living room and took the copy of *Brighton Rock* from my bag. It was a while since I'd had a good read.

CHAPTER SIXTEEN

Tor? A boy was standing in the shadows, holding a doll by the hair. The doll was wearing a blue dress.

What's her name? I asked.

Her name? Although he stepped out into the light I still couldn't see his face. *Why this is Mary the Mother of God.*

"Tor?" The voice hovered above my right ear. "Are you awake?" I opened my eyes and looked straight into Gareth's. They were the same shade as

185

April's. "Shh! Mum's asleep!" He clamped a finger across his lips.

Lucky Mum, and she'd been in bed hours ahead of me. "What's the time?" I whispered back.

"It's seven o'clock. You don't want to miss Rug Rats do you?"

I couldn't give a toss about Rug Rats, all I wanted to do was roll over and have a decent lie-in. "Gareth, Rug Rats doesn't come on till eight-thirty." Another hour and a half, I'd do anything for another hour and a half.

"I know." Desperation was seeping in. "But we need time to make toast. And hot chocolate, let's make hot chocolate. It's really cold."

I sat up on my elbows. "Why are you wearing only your pajamas?" I hissed. "Where's your dressing gown?"

"I didn't know how cold it was going to be when I got out of bed." This was accompanied by a shiver.

"Slippers? Where are your slippers?" I hung over the edge of the futon. His feet were bare. "You'll catch your death. You go and put your dressing gown and your slippers on."

He grinned hopefully. "And you'll make chocolate again? Really thick, like last time?"

It was no use, I was up. "Death-by-Chocolate it is," I said.

"Jurassic!" Giving a hushed whoop he ran from the room.

Out in the kitchen he was itching to do things properly. "No, not margarine," he said. "I'll get the butter."

I yawned. "Fine. You scrape the butter so it'll spread and I'll concentrate on the chocolate. I'm going to make this so thick a spoon will stand up in it."

"Ace!"

"And your teeth will fall out, one by one."

"I'm staying at my friend Dominic's place tonight, and we're going to play on his Sega Mega Drive."

"Uh-huh." I lifted the saucepan by the handle just as the milk tipped the rim. My timing was perfect.

"We play Sonic Hedgehog. And Jungle Strike." The way he said this last bit suggested I wasn't supposed to approve.

"Oh? What's that?" I sprinkled chocolate pieces over the froth in both mugs.

"You have to protect the White House against terrorists. You get to kill loads of people."

"Sounds charming."

"But you *have* to kill them you see. You're under orders to protect the President."

"That argument didn't work at Nuremberg, you know."

"What?"

I lightly cuffed his cropped hair, which was still standing with yesterday's gel. The application of the gel had recently become a morning ritual; he'd even had a go at my mousse. Almost double figures, almost a teenager. At fourteen I'd rebelled against the Saturday morning visits to the charity shops and accused my mother of buying things second-hand purely in order to embarrass me. What if Gareth turned on me one day, embarrassed by my relationship with April? What if he didn't want to live with us any more, and went back to his Dad? I quickly turned to the refrigerator and searched for jam.

"Tor?" He was getting out plates.

"Uh-huh."

"Thanks for getting up to have breakfast with me."

"Yeah, well I guess I must love Death-by-Chocolate as much as you do."

"So, it's a deal then?" The deal was that April was taking Gareth shopping for shoes, and then on to Dominic's. In the meantime I'd go back to Hoxton and sort out my kitchen.

I pulled on my coat. "It is."

"Because we're moving three weeks from today you know. That means we've only got two weekends left for packing." Her anxiety seemed entirely appropriate, although I was well aware that it was due not only to our imminent move but also to the bruise now turning yellow under my right eye. I'd offered her a laundered version of my encounter with Ted and the ghoulish Bronwyn.

"Don't worry, I'll have the kitchen done by the time you arrive tonight. Promise."

The kitchen wouldn't take long to sort out. Instead of bussing to Waterloo and heading home from there on the Tube I stayed on the bus to Charing Cross, then got on the Jubilee Line. St. John's Wood was only four stops. Outside the station a newspaper boy gave me grudging directions and soon after I was in the St. John's Wood Public Library. Before ringing Iris Rocke with the good news I had one last spot of research to do.

* * * * *

A twinge of panic went through me when I saw the listing in the electoral register: Samuel S. Smith, and Peregrine F. Charite. Where was Perry Alms? In front of me of course. And he didn't live alone. I giggled in relief and won a morose stare from a woman in a fluffy pink sweater. The giving of Alms, a charitable act. Replacing the register I went through to the library's Quick Reference section and pulled down a dictionary. *Alms: relief given out of pity; a charitable deed.* Flicking through the pages I came to charity, defined as *universal love; an alms-giver.* After *charity begins at home,* and *cold as charity,* was *charité,* the French origin. No doubt about it, I was on a winning streak.

I caught a taxi back to the flat, where a pile of junk mail awaited me inside the door. After binning the lot I made a cup of tea, then wandered through to check the answer machine. The first message was from Denise, saying she might, or might not, turn up later in the week. The second was from my friend Jeremy, announcing he'd rung in order to have a gossip and would get back to me some other time. The third message was from Jan; she'd discovered something about the Rocke family she thought I should know, could I ring her as soon as possible?

I certainly could, although I soon wished I hadn't.

"Are you sure?" I demanded, for the second time.

"Sure I'm sure. I'm an investigative journalist remember? I know a gangster's moll when I see one. The wedding photo on the social page is something else."

189

"And this was in seventy-two?"

"The gangland wedding of the year, I'd say. 'The bride, Louise Rocke, was resplendent in . . .' and so forth, and so on. The happy couple intended to settle in Spain. Although it doesn't say so here, of course, her new hubby was well-known as a laundry man, handling stolen money, and goods. Spain was a favorite haven for British crims in the Seventies, a deep tan and your own pool were badges of success."

"Well, this is news." It was, but right at the moment I wasn't sure of its implications. What I was sure of however, was a sudden itchiness in my left arm pit: something wicked this way comes. Either that or I was allergic to my new deodorant.

"It's interesting gossip, but it probably doesn't affect you too much. I haven't come across anything more about Bryton Rocke, or her bloke Charlie; however I do have one other little snippet that might interest you."

The itchiness spread. "Is it to do with the Krays?"

Jan snorted, "Will you forget the Krays? I haven't heard anything that links your clients with the Krays; those bonzos in the photos are probably just wanna-bes. Listen to this though: Iris Rocke is the real thing."

I tried to imagine what this might mean and drew a complete blank. "What are you talking about?"

"Iris Rocke . . ." Jan wasn't trying to hide the fact that she was enjoying this, ". . . was a highly respected con artist in her day. Her specialty was long-term frauds, and so talented was she that she got sent down only once, spending three months in Holloway Prison."

I saw a teacup tremble in its saucer, a carpet patterned with red and blue birds, a rosary. "Bullshit Jan, you've got the wrong Iris Rocke."

She ignored me and went on. "Here are my notes. Let's see ... Born into a well-known criminal family, her father owned a string of suspect racehorses and was a flamboyant gambler known throughout the States, as well as in various European capitals. Her brother ran nightclubs in London and Newcastle until the mid-Seventies. He died from a stroke in 1975 and police suspected that he had been handling money for the underworld up until then. Walter Rocke, Iris's spouse of some thirty years, was whispered to be *a*, if not *the*, Mr. Big. His name was linked with gun-running and illegal gambling, but although he was hauled in for questioning on numerous occasions nothing was ever pinned on him. His wife was considered, by some, to be the real brains behind the operation. After his death she apparently went into retirement and now lives in solitary splendor, though still served by one of her husband's faithful henchmen."

"Joseph," I added weakly. The gray man in the gray suit, Iris's secretary.

"Known as Jo the Knife in his heyday, although he actually preferred guns. Served three years for the manslaughter of a small-time burglar named Billy Gregor, who injudiciously insulted Mr. Rocke. On Jo's release from jail a fleet of three Rolls-Royces laden with roses, champagne and caviar, were sent to the prison gates to meet him."

I felt like I was swimming against a strong tide. "Jan, this just doesn't fit. Iris Rocke is a refined, very quiet woman. She's a staunch Catholic, for heaven's sake!"

"Since when have refined and quiet guaranteed good and honest? As for Catholic, why do you think she named her daughter after that novel? Have you read *Brighton Rock*, Tor?"

What did this have to do with anything? "I started on it last night." The truth was that I'd found it heavy going and after the second chapter had given up and watched a late-night nude chat show instead. Out of anthropological interest, of course.

"Well it seems to me your Mrs. Rocke does a nice line in irony. Pinkie, the boy gangster who the novel's about, is a Roman Catholic."

The boy holding the Mother of God by the hair.

"Oh."

"Tor, I think you should make very sure you know what these people are after. Look, I gotta run now but if you want to talk it through at any stage I'm here, remember that."

"I'll remember. And thank you, Jan."

He'd been very kind, Frankie had said, about the shells. Why does a kind man, a good man, change his name and disappear, unless he's afraid of someone? Cho believed the man in the blue suit had wanted to protect Perry. What if Iris Rocke was the person he needed protection from?

* * * * *

At eight o'clock the following morning I breakfasted on croissants and marmalade at King's Cross Station; by ten o'clock I was the Palace Pier's first customer of the day.

"Come to have your cards read, have you?" The woman unlocking the gates nodded sympathetically. "Does palms too, she does. And the leaves. Only the locals ask for the leaves, so she tells me, even though they give a better reading than the cards." As she swung the gate wide I was awarded an approving look. "It'll be bitter at the end but at least you're dressed for it. Had an American woman here yesterday, in a summer frock without even a cardigan. 'Aren't you cold?' I ask and she gives this big smile and says, 'I'm from Tallahassee.' What's that supposed to mean? Some of these tourists are completely barmy, they really are."

Underneath my boots the wooden boards of the pier were gritty with tar and sand, while from below, the rising tide brought with it the sound of scraping shingle. Forty-five feet high, that's what the sign at the entrance said, and fifteen hundred feet in length. Built in 1899, the Palace Pier was now Britain's largest funfair. Trailing my gloved fingers along the wooden handrail I walked past the first arcade, the Palace of Fun, and then a cluster of closed stalls advertising souvenirs, hot dogs, and Cornish pasties. Next came a cafe and the Pleasuredome.

Beyond the Pleasuredome was an old-fashioned helter skelter and as I glanced up at the peeling red and blue paintwork I remembered climbing a similar one as a child, and screaming in terror all the way down the spiral slide. Neither the helter skelter nor the ghost train looked as if they'd been in use since the summer. Opposite the ghost train the fortune teller's booth was plastered with the photos of celebrities who'd availed themselves of the services offered.

At the end of the Pier the breeze chopped the water into white-topped ridges and defied a desultory seagull's attempts to land on the handrails. Leaning against the rails myself, I looked back toward the shore, to where the Union Jacks fluttered above the entrance with all the aplomb of washing on a line. It had to be said that this was a completely inappropriate place to have an important meeting with a rich, elderly woman like Iris Rocke. And the more inappropriate it was, the more I liked it.

I was the cafe's only customer. A waitress wiped windows with a damp green cloth while I sipped tea and watched a lone angler hang over the outside rail threading worms onto a hook with deft fingers.

At ten-thirty exactly Iris Rocke walked through the door. "Miss Cross, here you are." She didn't smile, but then neither did I.

"Good morning." I pushed a metal chair out for her with my foot: a touch rude but not, as yet, insolent. "Would you like some tea Mrs. Rocke?" Where, I wondered, was Joseph? The silent gray man in the gray suit. Where was Jo the Knife this brisk winter morning?

"Coffee. Please."

I came back with black coffee and some sort of whitener in a plastic tub. Sorry madam, but we're out of fresh cream. Sorry I couldn't come to meet you in your grand house at the end of your grand drive, but I'm setting the agenda today. I was determined to milk my surroundings for all they were worth and had dressed for the occasion in tight black jeans and a heavy black sweater. As I scraped my hair back in front of the mirror this morning, a phrase had floated into my mind: pared to the bone. That's how I felt; that's how I wanted to feel.

A diamond pin glittered on the lapel of Iris's cashmere coat. "I gather that you have located Perry Alms." Her eyes didn't meet mine but focused on some distant point over the horizon; the two of us might have been in a rowing boat, a yacht. She'd removed her leather gloves and now her hands were lightly clasped on the table in front of her. On her left hand she wore a wedding ring.

When I'd rung her last night I hadn't told her in so many words that I'd found Perry, but I had dropped some pretty heavy hints. "As I said last night, Mrs. Rocke, I can't continue acting on your behalf until you tell me exactly why it is you want to locate him. I want the truth, and if I don't get it I'm not willing to go any further with this case. If you don't want to tell me, that's fine, I'll leave now and the agency will send you a final account."

The breeze had done some work on her hair and fine strands of gray clung to the side of her face; this was the nearest to disheveled I was ever likely to see her. Never, I reminded myself, trust a con artist. You cannot believe anything this woman says.

Turning her head to look at me she finally murmured, "You're right, I have been less than honest with you."

Well, that much was true. "I want it straight. From the beginning," I emphasized. "I want to know why your daughter hired me to find Perry Alms."

The hands rose for a minute as if in prayer, then fell back. She gave a faint smile. "I will tell you the whole story, Miss Cross."

I didn't reply and after a moment she continued. "You see it wasn't really Perry Alms that Bryton was hoping to find. She was actually looking for someone else."

Whatever I'd expected it wasn't this. If it wasn't Perry she was looking for, then who?

"Mrs. Rocke," I said carefully. "Who, or what, is it that you're after?"

Her eyes were a deep gray. "Bryton's grandchild," she said. "I want to find my great-granddaughter."

Outside the window the fisherman took the hook from the mouth of a small silver fish, which he then threw back into the water. Fifty-six, *The Observer* article had given Bry's age as fifty-six. I could have checked that easily enough if I'd wanted. If I'd thought. "How old is Louise?" I asked.

Picking up the tub of whitener she used a fingernail to peel off the plastic film top. "Louise is forty-two," she replied. "Bryton hadn't turned fifteen when Louise was born." She stirred her coffee without looking at me. "This is a long story, Miss Cross. I hope you don't mind?"

I shook my head. Indeed I didn't.

"Bryton," her mother reminisced, "wasn't wild, but she was intense. In her early teens she was passionate about things, including religion. I know many girls go through a religious stage but I really did think she might become a nun. At the convent they definitely thought she had the beginnings of a vocation. And then, at fourteen, she was pregnant. The father was a young Irish priest, who was sent back to Dublin immediately. Louise was brought up as Bryton's sister."

Behind Iris the waitress used her cloth to clean a board for today's menu. Gangsters. The waitress's white arm performed a slow arc, as if she were waving to someone.

"Bryton's father and I were very worried about what to do with her next," Iris said. "She was completely devoted to Louise but was also emotionally unstable, laughing one minute, in floods of tears the next. My husband was concerned that she was going to have a complete breakdown and he decided the best thing was for Bryton to be sent away. So, against my wishes, he arranged for her to live in London with my brother and his family. My brother owned three clubs in London and she worked in them, closely supervised of course." Putting her spoon down she absently ran a fingertip around the chipped edge of an ashtray. "My husband was right, it was the best thing for her."

"Does Louise know?" I asked. The waitress was writing on the board. *Soup of The Day*, she wrote, *Mushroom*.

"We told her when she was twelve. Bryton hoped Louise would begin to relate to her as her mother, but she never did. Instead she insisted that no one else was to know, and she continued treating Bryton as an older sister. Bryton was terribly hurt, but Louise's reaction was understandable in a child of that age. I didn't find it so understandable when she was an adult."

What would it be like, to be suddenly told your mother was your grandmother, your sister was your mother?

Iris was watching my face. "Louise was very different from Bryton, more restrained, less intense. We had no problems with her at all. And then, at sixteen, she announced she was leaving home and going to live in London. Which is exactly what she did. I have no idea where she went to live, or how she supported herself. I know Bryton gave her money whenever she turned up to ask for it."

"So this was when?" I asked. " 'Sixty-nine?" Was it because she was pregnant that she'd left?

Iris undid the front of her coat and reached for her bag. "Do you mind if I smoke?" I shook my head and she pulled out cigarettes and a silver lighter. "It was 'Sixty-eight. Louise maintained fairly regular contact with Bryton but then Bryton and Charlie opened their club here and there was no word from Louise at all, except for a couple of cryptic postcards. Bryton was frantic about Louise, and at the same time Charlie was having problems with his heart."

"Was Louise pregnant at this stage?"

She held the burning cigarette back from the table. "Yes, but we didn't know that. She suddenly reappeared down here as if nothing had happened. Bryton was completely thrilled to have her back, but my husband had had enough. Walter had many contacts in London and he was determined to discover where Louise had been living, and what she'd been up to."

The fingers of her left hand tucked a strand of hair back into place. "I'll never forget the evening he arrived home and told me he'd discovered that

Louise had had a baby. My husband had a very strong sense of family, and of family pride, Miss Cross. He hadn't been pleased when Bryton fell pregnant, but he did respect the fact that she'd had the guts to tell him herself, and that she wanted to keep her child. He could not understand Louise's secrecy. He confronted her that night and demanded she tell him what she had done with her baby. She said she'd had a girl, and that although she'd split up with her boyfriend his family was bringing the child up. She refused to say who the father was."

"How did Bryton react to this?" And who was the father? Was she saying that Perry Alms was the father of Louise's child?

"We didn't tell her. Charlie had had to go back to manage the London club and was soon seriously ill. Bryton was in a terrible state."

The coffee had washed faint trails of color into the cracks around her lips, and her mouth was old under the bright eyes. I looked at her and tried to remember what it was Bryton had said about not returning to London. Her father had died shortly before Charlie, and she'd stayed on to be close to her mother. How did Iris's story fit in with this?

"Mrs. Rocke, when did your husband die?" I asked.

She nodded, as if the question was expected. "The week after he found out about Louise. He'd spent the day in London again. I remember coming home and finding Joseph parking the car in the garage, they'd only just arrived. I walked into the house and heard Louise and my husband having an argument upstairs. Walter was yelling at Louise, using language I'd never heard him use to the girls before.

As I walked through to see what was happening Louise screamed. Walter's body was at the foot of the stairs; he'd stepped backwards and fallen."

"I see."

"You don't." She shook her head. "It's a hard time in a woman's life to be left alone, Miss Cross. You look ahead and you see twenty, possibly thirty, years stretching in front of you."

A seagull perched on the edge of a litter bin outside the window and fixed me with a black eye. Where did Perry Alms fit into all this?

"And Perry?"

She sipped at what must have been lukewarm coffee. "I didn't tell Bryton about the baby. I felt that Louise had made her own decision, and the matter was best left alone. Some years later, however, I ran into Phillip Haine, an old business associate of my husband, and he told me that Walter had visited him that last day in London. Walter had asked Phillip to find out what he could about the father of Louise's child. When I met him again Phillip couldn't remember the name of her boyfriend, but what he did remember was that Louise hadn't given the baby up to her boyfriend's family at all. She had, in fact, sold it."

"Good God." I couldn't help it.

Iris tilted her head to one side. "It's a dark world ours, don't you think, Miss Cross? Man makes it dark, at any rate. And woman too." For a moment her mouth was cavernous, ancient. "Louise sold her daughter to Perry Alms."

Underneath the pier the tide was rising. "How old will she be now?" I speculated aloud. "Twenty-four, almost twenty-five?"

"My great-granddaughter is a young woman. By the time I heard about Perry Alms, Louise had married and was living in Spain. Bryton and I rarely heard from her, and she always discouraged the possibility of Bryton ever paying a visit. In fact we hadn't seen her for ten years before she came back here to live, eighteen months ago. She rang one day to say her husband had been killed in a car crash and she had decided to return. I must say I was extremely surprised."

"How did Bryton react when you told her about her grandchild?" How would you feel about a daughter who could sell her baby?

"Bryton knew nothing about the child until just before Christmas. It had become clear that she might not have much longer to live and I felt it was her right to know. She was terribly excited at the news."

For the first time Iris Rocke's voice wavered. "Bryton felt this was an opportunity for Louise to get to know her child. She wanted, very much, before she died, to see 'Louise reunited with her daughter. I encouraged her but without, I'm afraid, disclosing my real reasons for wanting to meet my great-granddaughter. Unlike Bryton, I was under no illusion that Louise would fall into her daughter's arms, but I was aware that Bryton's death would leave me without an heir. I have no intention of leaving my estate to Louise. So there you have the truth, Miss Cross."

I believed her. I believed her completely. But then I'd also believed Bry had lost a museum piece, and that Perry Alms was about to hit the jackpot. I looked around to where two other tables now had

201

seated customers. Three teenage boys laughed and drank coffee a few tables from us; beside the door, a middle-aged couple doled out plates of chocolate cake among their offspring.

"Why didn't you, or Bry, tell me the truth from the start?"

"In my family, Miss Cross, we have always handled private matters ourselves."

Once upon a time, maybe, but these days Iris's family was somewhat thin on the ground. I glanced down to the floor, where the toes of my black leather boots were neatly lined up against each other. A well-respected con artist, I reminded myself. Who'd served time in Holloway. Walter wasn't a businessman on a day trip to London, he was a Mr. Big. Daughter Louise had married a gangster and Joseph wasn't simply the chauffeur, polishing the car out in the drive. Bry had run an illegal casino. The story I'd just listened to hadn't included any of this colorful background material.

"Miss Cross." Her voice was oddly formal. "Please tell me. Have you found Perry Alms?"

Perry Alms, the good man. Perry Alms, accepting the wafer from the priest's hand: I had a sudden picture of him on a beach composed of glistening white shells.

"Yes," I said. "I have found him, Mrs. Rocke. But I'm not going to tell you where he is."

The look Iris Rocke leveled at me was a mixture of exasperation, and anger. I'd like to think that in comparison I appeared quietly confident.

CHAPTER SEVENTEEN

I caught the one o'clock train back to Victoria Station, took the Victoria line to Green Park and then changed onto the Jubilee. Emerging from the Baker Street Tube two stops later, I ignored the signs recommending a visit to the London Planetarium and Madame Tussaud's and headed instead in the direction of the Marylebone Reference Library. A local library like that at St. John's Wood wouldn't carry back copies of the electoral register, but here, I knew, they began from 1950.

Seven years. If Iris Rocke was telling the truth,

her great-granddaughter would have been able to register as a voter seven years ago, when she was eighteen.

I worked my way along the shelves, found the volume I wanted, and leafed through to the St. John's Wood address. In 1987 three people were registered at that address: they were Peregrine Charite, Samuel Smith, and Mercy Rocke.

"Your For Sale sign has been nicked," April informed me.

"Shit." Walking across to the window I pulled the curtain and stared out into the darkness.

"You won't be able to see anything Victoria. Besides, there isn't anything *to* see."

That wretched boy from the vegetable shop. "I'll have to ring the agent."

"I already have. I told them the pole had gone too and they said they'll put a new one up sometime this week. They probably won't bother, you'll have to keep chivying them."

"Thank you."

April was packing books and I was wrapping glassware in newspaper. "So what happens next?" she asked.

"The stuff on the mantelpiece I think, don't you?" Although there were still a lot of books to do and we didn't have that many cardboard boxes.

A ball of newspaper hit my shoulder. "With your case, Victoria. Come on, it's all you've been thinking about all evening. What's your story going to be when you get them on the phone?"

Much to my surprise they weren't ex-directory and there was a number under Samuel Smith's name in the phone book. "Research," I said, to myself as much as to April. I'd been dithering about what approach to take ever since I'd got home. The research story was as good as any.

"Really?"

"Yep. At this stage I just want to find out where she is, then I'll think about what to do next."

"Research into what?"

"Oh, young women and education." While at the reference library I'd checked through all the registers for the past seven years and found Mercy had lived at home until she was twenty-one, which suggested she'd been studying for a degree. After that only Perry and Samuel Smith's names were listed. Where, I wondered, was the youngest Ms. Rocke living these days?

"And then what? You can't appear on her doorstep and simply break the news that Mummy was a gangster's moll, Grandma was murdered only last week in a gambling feud and Great-Grandma was a well-known crook in her day."

"She might know about her background, Perry might have told her." I forced the corners of a cardboard box lid under each other. "I'll play it by ear; Iris has given me carte blanche."

"It doesn't sound as if you gave her much choice."

"I didn't. I wasn't about to hand Perry Alms over when it was quite possible she'd been bullshitting me again."

"It's not only Perry you'd be handing over, but Mercy too," she reminded me.

I didn't need reminding.

After we'd filled all the available boxes April went to have a bath and I rang the St. John's Wood number. A man answered.

"Hello." I was more nervous than I'd expected. "I wonder if you can help me? I'm doing research into women and education and I'm anxious to contact Miss Mercy Rocke. Is she still living at that address?"

There was silence for a moment and then the murmur of voices in the background.

"Hello." A different man was speaking now. "I believe you're looking for Mercy?"

"Yes," I burbled, "Mercy Rocke. I'm doing some research into women and education you see and —"

He cut in, gently. "We have been expecting someone to contact us. Our daughter isn't here tonight but she will be home for lunch tomorrow. Would you like to come here to meet her, Miss . . ."

"Cross. Victoria Cross," I heard myself say. What did he mean, they'd been expecting someone to get in contact? Why was he inviting me over?

"This is Perry Charite, Miss Cross. Would early tomorrow afternoon be convenient for you? Say two o'clock?"

Anchee had rung earlier to say I had an eleven o'clock appointment with Glen, the man who'd received the blackmail threats, but as far as I knew she hadn't put me down for anything in the afternoon. "Fine," I said, "two will be fine."

"I'm sure Mercy will be only too happy to listen to whatever you have to say. We would invite you to lunch but Mercy is only in this country for a short visit, so we'd like to have her to ourselves for a little while."

He knew. But what? What did he know?

"Thank you, Mr. Charite." My voice was meek because that's exactly how I felt. "I'll look forward to meeting all of you tomorrow."

It was only when I got off the phone that I realized just how exhausted I was.

CHAPTER EIGHTEEN

Glen's wife was small with graying hair and worried eyes. "My husband has told me that he did sleep with this young woman, Miss Cross."

Very wise too, I thought. The best way to fight blackmail is to own up. So why were they here? Dump the letters in the bin, folks, that's all you have to do. Get yourselves a silent telephone number. I caught a glimpse of my reflection in the window. For this afternoon's appointment I'd dressed in a black, light wool suit; checking my earlobes I confirmed there were two neat gold studs in each. I tried to imagine what Mercy Rocke would be like. How long had she lived overseas? What did she do for a living?

Glen nodded. "Miriam has been wonderful." They were holding hands. "Far more forgiving than I deserve."

"That's great, it really is. Sometimes these things can bring people even closer together." You're paying for my time guys, what's your problem?

"The problem is . . ." Miriam shifted on the edge of her chair. "Glen has received another anonymous letter, threatening to tell my father."

Who owned the company Glen worked for. I could see that might cause difficulties.

"And our daughters," Glen took off his glasses and wiped his eyes. I reached behind me for the box of Kleenex I keep at hand for these moments. "Thank you. Our eldest girl is going through a very difficult time, and if she knew I'd been unfaithful . . ." He broke down and sobbed.

"Right." I reached for a notepad. "The first thing we need to do is obtain a copy of this woman's normal handwriting."

At five past two I parked Lucy and pulled down the sunguard to check my face in the mirror. I ran a comb through my fringe, quickly blotted my nose and smeared some gloss across my lips. I was excited, and nervous. I wanted to meet these people, I wanted to hear their story. But would they want to hear mine?

"Miss Cross, please come in." He gripped my

hand firmly, at the same time ushering me into an entrance hall. "I'm Samuel Smith."

Samuel Smith was the man from the newspaper photo. My heart did a slight lurch. He and Perry had been together over twenty-five years! His hair was gray and a pair of gold-rimmed glasses hung from a chain around his neck. He pointed down to a pair of worn, brown slippers, "Please forgive my informality but I've been having trouble with my feet. Do you do a lot of walking in your job, Miss Cross?"

Which job were we talking about? As a researcher into women's education, or as a hired snoop? I hedged my bets. "I like walking a lot."

He nodded approvingly. "People don't use Shanks's pony enough, I'm always telling Perry that. But I shouldn't be keeping you out here, please come through to the living room."

A glossy palm in a terracotta pot filled the large bay window while the olive walls were decorated with bright paintings and hangings. "From Nicaragua." Samuel had followed my look. "And Mexico. Now please sit down." He gestured toward an enormous leather sofa in front of a low coal fire. "Mercy and Perry are dealing with the dishwasher. I'll let them know you're here."

I stood up again as soon as he left the room, partly because I was too nervous to sit, and partly so that I could inspect the framed photographs on the mantelpiece. The young woman standing between Samuel and Perry wore a white shirt and denim jeans and had short dark hair. All three people were smiling in what I assumed was a holiday snap, taken against a background of exotic flowering trees. In another photo the same young woman, this time with shoulder-length hair, posed formally in an academic gown and mortar board. I picked up the photo, puzzled that although she looked vaguely familiar, her dark hair and eyes didn't remind me of any of the women in the Rocke family. Whom did she remind me of? Was it Perry? Could he be her real father after all?

"Hello there."

Swinging around I almost dropped the picture. "Good heavens!"

My exclamation was greeted with a loud laugh. "You're right there," she agreed.

Mercy Rocke was a nun.

"I'm a Salesian Sister," she explained. "At home I don't always wear this, though. It's not terribly practical."

"This" was a heavy gray habit and home was an orphanage in Romania, where she'd now been living for six months. Before that she'd spent two years working in a hospital in Nicaragua.

Mercy had seated herself comfortably between me and Samuel on the sofa. Perry occupied an armchair in the corner and although he'd greeted me with a warm smile he'd remained silent. A good man, yes, but also a complicated one. A religious man who'd worked as a nightclub manager; a gay man who'd wanted a child and had been willing to give up his public identity in order to keep her.

I caught his eye. "I expect you're wondering why I'm here," I offered.

He shook his head. "We do know you're not

211

really here to do research Miss Cross, because we'd been told that someone was asking questions. We were expecting a visit of some sort."

Told by whom? Surely not by Ted? Mercy lightly touched my knee. "Is it my mother who's looking for me?" she asked. She sounded interested, but not desperately so. I had the feeling that Mercy Rocke had her life fairly well worked out and the fact that her mother had dumped her as a baby was neither here nor there.

"I'm employed by Iris Rocke," I said. "Bryton Rocke hired me to look for you in the first place, but unfortunately she died very recently."

Samuel sat forward. "We saw in the newspaper that she'd been shot. A very sad business." He sounded genuinely sad, but not greatly surprised.

"I was always fond of Bryton," Perry said. "She was a very warm person. I often wished Mercy could have known her as she was growing up, but . . ."

He didn't have to explain. Contact with Bryton would have meant contact with Louise. Samuel and Perry must have constantly worried that Louise would one day make a reappearance, either wanting her daughter back, or demanding more money.

I turned to Mercy. "Iris Rocke would very much like to meet you." Wouldn't she ever, her great-granddaughter, a nun! "Did you know she's a Catholic too?" I asked.

Mercy nodded. "Perry told me that."

"I was talking to Iris yesterday morning and she said that Bryton had thought about becoming a nun when she was very young." I almost blurted out that her grandfather had been a priest as well, but managed to restrain myself. Iris could tell her that, if Mercy agreed to meet her. Below the gray habit her black shoes were thick-soled and sensible. Looking at them I found myself wondering if vocation might be a hereditary matter.

Samuel's pride in Mercy was obvious. "I'm not religious myself, Miss Cross," he said. "But I have always been impressed by our daughter's determination in this matter. Perry and I insisted that she go to university first and although she was a good student, and enjoyed her time at the university, her desire to join a religious order never wavered."

I was dying to ask what it was like for a nun to have been brought up by two gay men. What did she tell the sisters back at the convent?

"My aunt's death must have left my grandmother very alone." Mercy was looking thoughtful. Not your aunt, I thought, your grandmother. I noticed that she didn't seem to hold any illusions about her own mother, Louise.

I nodded. "I think it has. She asked me to invite you down to Brighton, if you're willing to meet her. She suggested I might come with you." I gave her time to think this over by asking Perry a question. "By the way, who told you I'd been making enquiries?"

"Tony," he replied, "who went as far as following you I believe." He raised his palms in a gesture of apology.

I wasn't about to confess to Perry that I'd gone as far as to watch him taking communion. Tony must be the man in the blue suit. I remembered the photo of him looking in through the restaurant window, and suddenly realized who Mercy reminded me of. "Tony," I said, "is he . . . ?"

Mercy nodded. "Tony's my father. My biological father," she added. "He traced Perry and Samuel last year. I met him just before I went to Romania."

"Yes," said Samuel. "The Abbess came and dined with Mercy's three fathers. She coped very well, I thought. But then, she's from Bucharest." This was said as if it explained all. It probably did.

CHAPTER NINETEEN

At nine-fifteen on Wednesday morning Miss Williams, the young lady with whom Glen had had his flingette, was at her post at the reception desk of a public relations company based in Fulham.

"Excuse me, are you Miss Williams?" Her hands were resting on the desk and I did a quick check. Excellent, just as Glen had said; fingernail extensions.

"That's right." She gave me a cursory glance. "Do you have an appointment?"

"It's actually you I'm here to see."

"Oh." The black folder tucked neatly under my arm was awarded a nervous glance; maybe I was a new face from personnel. Her manner brightened. "How can I help you, Mrs. . . . ?"

My advanced age must have won me this sign of respect. "Stallman," I replied. "Cheryl Stallman." I lowered my voice. "To tell the truth I'm hoping you'll be able to help me, Miss Williams. I'm doing market research on nailcare products and I'm looking for young businesswomen who are conscious of how vital hand care is in creating a well-groomed appearance." I just hate myself at times.

She glanced down at her hands. "Well it's true that I do look after my nails, but I really don't have time to . . ."

"We're very much aware that in business these days time means money, so we do offer a fee of ten pounds to those who are kind enough to help us. The questionnaire doesn't take long to fill in at all." I whipped open the folder and waved two sheets of A4 in front of her. "There are some basic questions here that only require a couple of sentences each. I'm authorized to pay the ten pounds on completion of the questionnaire. In cash, of course."

"Really?" A fingernail almost made it into her mouth, but she caught herself in time. "Well if you leave one with me I'll fill it out tonight."

I hugged the folder across my chest. "That's what I'd normally do, but I'm afraid I'm in a bit of a fix. I was supposed to get these finished yesterday and my boss doesn't know I'm a day behind. She'll be furious if she finds out. I'm hoping I'll come across enough women who'll be able to complete the questionnaires this morning. But if you don't have time I quite understand, I've got some other names here."

"I can do it now, I suppose." She wasn't going to watch ten quid walk down the hall that easily.

"Thank you very much. I'll deliver the rest of these and then call back."

"Yeah." She peered at the first question. "But I won't be able to type it you know, I don't have a typewriter out here."

"Oh don't worry about that. Handwritten answers are more than acceptable, Miss Williams."

I left her laboring over her answers and took myself around the corner to a cafe where I had bagels and coffee for breakfast and started reading the latest *Time Out*.

"Morning!"

Anchee looked at her watch. "Lunch time is what the rest of the world calls it."

"Speaking of which, Gino's done a take-away for me." I balanced the flat cardboard box on the tips of my fingers, trying to avoid the grease that had already soaked through the bottom. "Quatro fromage. That's ricotta, gorgonzola, mozzarella and dolcelatte. You wanna slice?"

"There's no garlic?" Her sniff was suspicious.

How someone can hoover through vast quantities of ginger and then balk at the merest hint of garlic is beyond me. "None whatsoever."

"Okay, I'll help you out."

"And then I've got handwriting samples to compare so I'd appreciate it if you stopped any calls for me."

"I know, I know, you *artistes* need to concentrate." She started to refill a stapler and I turned towards my door. "Before you go . . ."

"Uh-huh." I wanted to put this pizza down and wipe my hand.

"I've got news." The stapler jammed and she used a ballpoint pen to flick open the end.

"Good or bad?"

"All good."

Anchee with nothing but good news? The clients must have been prompt with this month's checks. "Lay it on me."

"The feminist publishers have agreed to two car spaces."

"Brilliant! What did you do, promise we'd all join their book club?"

"And our boss rang to say she'll be back next week."

Alicia would soon be back! Jesus, I'd missed that woman. I danced the pizza into my office.

Miss Williams had made a crude attempt to disguise her handwriting in the letters to Glen, but comparing them with the fake questionnaire, there was no doubt the letters were in her hand. Which meant I'd be calling on her again tomorrow morning. After showing her my comparison of the documents I'd take great pleasure in informing her how confident I was that this evidence would stand up in court. Threatening to tell tales to a man's teenage daughters, dear dear, no jury was going to like that. Miss Williams, I knew, would be panicking by this point, and I had every intention of turning the screw as tightly as possible. In my first year at the agency, one of Alicia's clients had committed suicide as the result of being blackmailed, and since then I'd regarded blackmail as one of the cruelest trades, a blend of viciousness and cowardice. Holding the tracing-paper graphs I'd made up to the light, I contemplated the beautifully regular pattern created by her ascending and descending strokes. Yes indeed, I was going to make Miss Williams squirm...

"Tor!" Anchee's head appeared around the door.

Five more minutes, that's all I needed. "I'm not quite —"

"There's someone here to see you."

Shit. "Can I just have —"

"It's him!" Diane was leaning over Anchee's shoulder. "Tor," she hissed, "he's here!"

"Who?" I hissed back.

"The bloke who followed you last week, he's waiting outside to see you."

No he wasn't, he was standing at the end of the queue. "Hello." I stood up and held out my hand. "You're Tony aren't you? I'm Tor Cross, please come in."

The man in the blue suit. Today, however, he was wearing a dark sports jacket and a rust polo shirt. His handshake was firm, but not what you'd call friendly.

"What I want to confirm, Miss Cross, is that you have contacted my daughter on behalf of Iris Rocke, and not Louise."

"I explained all this to Mercy yesterday."

He dismissed this with a wave of his hand. "Miss Cross, my daughter, and Perry and Samuel, are only too willing to believe good about people. They are good people themselves. But I know what sort of woman Louise is. I know she is quite capable of trying to abuse their generosity and that she would happily hire some grubby private detective to do her dirty work for her."

Who are you to talk, I thought. "You let Louise sell Mercy in the first place," I said.

He stared at me, then relaxed and laughed. Laughing, he had Mercy's dark eyes and generous mouth. "You've got me there, although I should say that I didn't know Louise was pregnant until after I'd dumped her. But when I did hear she was pregnant, and had made a financial deal with a wealthy homosexual couple, do you know what my reaction was?"

I shook my head. I didn't know at all.

He clapped his hands. "That. I respected ruthlessness back then, you see. I was young, and aspiring to be a hard man. But when it came to jail I soon learned I wasn't hard enough." He shrugged. "After getting out I cleaned up my act and for twenty years have been an honest, and successful, businessman. But that doesn't mean I'm weak, Miss Cross. Believe me, I'm not."

I believed him.

He went on. "By chance I ran into Louise in a wine bar after she'd come back from Spain. Seeing Louise made me think about the child I'd never met. I have lost one child already Miss Cross, I lost my son to heroin three years ago. I failed my son, and my wife divorced me. I've already failed my daughter once, but I won't fail her again. I'll do whatever I have to to protect her. I think you should know that."

I thought I should too.

So that's it, I told myself after he'd left. I'd met all the main contenders, all the pieces were in place. There was still the question of exactly who was responsible for Bry's murder, of course, but the police were responsible for that part of the puzzle.

"Well?" Diane burst through the door.

"Well what?"

"Did you explain everything to him? He looked serious Tor, so I hope you cleared up any misunderstandings."

I hoped so. I'd stressed that Iris had hired me and that it was only natural she should want to contact her great-grandchild. To which Mercy's father had replied that the Rocke women weren't known for their naturalness. I also said that Mercy seemed a pretty strong personality and that I doubted she'd succumb to Louise's wiles if they did happen to meet. Tony left looking slightly happier. All the same, he was desperately protective of his new-found daughter and he wasn't someone I'd particularly want to annoy.

"So?" Diane demanded.

"So she's a nun with three fathers and they worry about her." I shrugged. "It happens."

April didn't immediately jump at the offer of a trip to Brighton but throughout the evening I attempted to construct a convincing argument on the grounds that these days we only met over the top of a cardboard box. "We can spend Friday morning going around the junk shops, and the second-hand bookshops."

"You mean the second-hand clothes shops." She was sorting through my old sheets.

"Those too. Come on, you've only got one lecture on Friday. It'll be fun. I'll treat you to high tea at the Royal Pavilion." As far as I was concerned the selling point was the thought of tomorrow night spent in a hotel bedroom and not a cardboard box in sight. "We can catch the five o'clock train down and arrive in time for dinner. I can claim my half on expenses."

"You're on," she said.

Two hours later we were both tired and dusty and April went off to have the first bath. I was lying on the sofa, leafing through my undergraduate copy of *Songs of Innocence and Experience*, when the phone rang.

"It's me, Tor." It was Jan.

"Listen to this, 'Pity no more could be, If all were as happy as we.' That was written exactly two hundred years ago."

"And what have we learned in the meantime? Now do you want to hear my latest, or not?"

Something about her voice made me suspect I didn't. "Shoot."

"Louise Rocke." Jan wasn't speaking into the mouthpiece. "Excuse me but I'm pouring myself a drink."

"What about Louise?"

"Well, you remember I said she'd been gangland bride of the year? My friend Paula is researching a

222

book and at the moment she's investigating the crims who left the U.K. and went into semi-retirement in Spain. I've asked her about Ms. Rocke and apparently her name crops up quite often. She's never been charged with anything, but it's widely rumored that over the years she's acted as a go-between for various drug barons and the Italian Mafia."

"Drugs?" I tossed Blake onto the carpet and sat up.

"Hard ones, not soft. Stuff coming through from Turkey. Her husband is thought to have organized the transport of large quantities of cocaine throughout Europe, that is until he fell down his staircase and broke his neck. The funeral was attended by —"

"Hold on, can you run that past me again?" On the mantelpiece Denise's figurines peeped knowingly from under their parasols.

There was the clunk of glass against the receiver. "Which bit?"

"The bit where he falls down the stairs and breaks his neck."

"What about it?"

"Are you sure that's how he died? The way Louise told it to Iris, he was killed in a car accident."

"I don't think so because Paula translated a report from a Spanish newspaper over the phone. If I remember rightly the soon-to-be-widowed Louise was frolicking out in the pool when she heard an alarming thud. Running inside she was distraught to find her husband's crumpled body at the bottom of the stairs." Her husband Walter had been arguing with Louise, and he'd stepped backwards, Iris Rocke had said. He'd stepped backwards and fallen.

"Tor, you will tell me if you stumble across a story, won't you?"

"Yes. Of course, Jan." But there was someone else I had to tell first.

When I'd rung Iris the previous night to tell her that her great-granddaughter was a nun, and that she was willing to come to dinner on Friday, her response had been quietly jubilant. She could hardly be blamed for thinking years of prayer had paid off. Tonight, however, she listened to what I had to say in silence.

"Mrs. Rocke? It's possible that the reports in the Spanish papers aren't true. Or Louise may have had a good reason for not wanting to tell you how her husband really died." I could think of a very good reason indeed.

"Thank you." Her voice was calm. "Thank you for warning me, Miss Cross. In fact the police have been to talk to me today. Louise hasn't been seen since Monday and they are becoming very concerned."

Louise, a woman standing on a veranda under a tropical sky. Maybe that's what she was doing right now. Maybe.

As I put the phone down April emerged from the bathroom, toweling her hair. She yawned. "You'd better go for it while it's still hot. You know this trip to Brighton is a good idea, Victoria, we could both do with a break. It should be great fun."

"Yes," I said. "It should."

CHAPTER TWENTY

On Thursday British Rail was hit by random industrial action and late in the afternoon I had to dash to Heathrow Airport with a witness order. The result of all this was that April and I weren't on either the five, or six o'clock trains to Brighton. We did make it onto the seven o'clock, and by ten we'd dined in the hotel restaurant and were back in our room.

"Champagne!" She laughed in delight.

"But of course." I'd smuggled it out of my overnight bag and onto our balcony before we went down to dinner. "Ice-cold." I handed her a glass, "To us."

"To the future." Her breasts were silhouettes under the soft black sweater. Kicking off her shoes she tucked her feet under her on the wide sofa. "Where do you think all those people were going?" The Albion's dining room had been full of women in long evening dresses, men in dinner suits.

"To the Theatre Royal, for the opera." I ran my finger around the rim of my glass and it began a low hum. "I think they were going to see Madam Butterfly."

Tell me a story. A story about a woman in a kimono, her eyes blue flowers.

"I think they were movie extras. I think that if we went out onto the balcony we'd see the Pier set up with lights and cameras and all those people would be waltzing slowly up and down."

This is our special game, the fantasy game. Vignettes handed back and forth like a familiar nosegay. I didn't look at April but at the glass I was holding. "With the waves splashing across the boards and gusts of snow."

"At the end of the Pier two women walk hand-in-hand out from the shadows. One puts her arm around the other's waist. Slowly they begin to dance, the music coming in faint bursts above the sound of water surging below."

The woman with blue eyes tilts her head back and parts her lips.

"They stand against the giant slide and one of the women leans back, the wood rough against the tips of her fingers. Through half-closed eyes she sees the long swoop of lights from the shore and then her silk dress is being pulled up, very slowly. A hand cups her between her legs and she moves into it."

"And the other woman's voice says, your breasts, I want to see your breasts, and the thin strap of her dress is slipped down and her nipple is cold, and she's pushed back against the wood. The fingers slipping inside her are wet."

"April . . ." Blue eyes, blue as a winter sea. ". . . my love, come here."

We'd fallen out of bed late, brunched at a greasy spoon, and were now doing the rounds of the second-hand book and clothes shops.

"Victoria, you can't!" She took a closer look. "Can you?"

I didn't see why not. "Why not? It doesn't show my tits." I swirled around in front of the mirror. The dress was vintage Fifties, wine velvet with a flowered net panel in the front and a beaded neckline. It was unashamedly *kitsch* and I liked it. I liked it a lot.

April continued to look doubtful. "Lean forward."

"April, the net ends before my cleavage even begins. Or where my cleavage would begin if I had one."

"Go on, lean forward."

The sales assistant popped her head around the curtain and threw me a professional look. "You could always wear a low-cut bra."

"I could, but I don't need to. I'm completely decent." I leaned forward and shimmied my shoulders. "See?"

April grunted dubiously; the assistant gave a nod. "She'll do," she reassured April. "It's one of the benefits of a neat bustline."

"A neat bustline? Did you hear that?" I asked when we were alone again. "I'm not completely flat-chested then."

"No." April started rehanging dresses on their hangers. "Just mammogenically challenged."

We went on a guided tour of the Royal Pavilion and then treated ourselves to high tea in the adjoining Queen Adelaide Tearoom, overlooking the gardens.

"He was a right shit, wasn't he?" April spooned strawberry jam next to the cream on her plate.

"Who?" From somewhere beyond the garden came a faint peal of church bells.

"George the Fourth. Not a very nice man."

"A complete wanker, but I can't help but admire his taste in interior decor. Those blue and red dragons! And the ceilings, can you imagine how long it took to put on all that gold leaf?"

"Seven years." April was reading from the pamphlet. " 'First completed in 1787, it was rebuilt during the years 1815–1822 in the Indian style, with extravagant Chinese interiors. The architect, John Nash, created the most exotic building in Britain as the King's summer palace, and Brighton became the most fashionable of British resorts, frequented by the wealthy and famous.' " Putting the book down she reached for a scone. "Let's bring Gareth here in the spring. He'd love these teas."

"He'd adore the Pier."

Outside the window the lawn was slate gray under a thin sheet of ice. First built in 1787: I imagined women in stitched leather boots crunching across this same lawn, women in long coats and veiled hats. Their breath came in clouds and they clapped gloved hands together, hurrying to get in out of the cold. My imagined figures merged into real ones and as a long scarlet coat approached the glass my heart began to pound.

Louise? What was Louise doing here? A face peered in through the window and a woman with short salt-and-pepper hair shook her head at her companion, they'd try somewhere else.

"Victoria." Across the table April was wearing a pair of amethyst earrings we'd found at a shop in the Lanes. Her cheeks, and the tip of her nose, were pink.

"My love?" Louise wasn't still in Brighton, Louise was somewhere far, far away.

"I'm very glad we came down here. And I'm glad you didn't give up on this case. I was just being paranoid."

Paranoia has its place. "You were right to be worried. After all, Bry was murdered and I was very lucky I didn't gate-crash the event."

She shivered. "Do you think they'll catch the murderer?"

Bry, the unwilling murderee, a vine spreading across her chest. "I hope so," I said. "I really do hope so."

April caught the six o'clock train back to London and I was left on platform one, awaiting Mercy.

I didn't think much of the uniform, and celibacy

was a definite drawback, but those things aside, being a nun in the Nineties seemed a reasonable career option, if Mercy's career was anything to judge by. She'd spent the past two days at a conference in Milton Keynes in order, so she'd informed me over the phone, to deliver a paper entitled, *Is Marxism the Life-Blood of Liberation Theology? The View from Transylvania.* Tomorrow afternoon she was off to Brussels for a meeting with some bigwig in the European Parliament. All this, and no need whatsoever to worry about a personal pension.

Her gray bags matched her habit. I took one from her and said that Joseph would be waiting outside.

"He's my grandmother's secretary, right?"

"Right." If for grandmother you read great-grandmother, and for secretary, ex hit-man. Not a slow walker myself, I was striding to keep up with Mercy Rocke. They must walk really fast in Bucharest.

The Rolls wasn't decked out with baskets of goodies from Harrods but Joseph was wearing an extremely sharp black suit, complete with red carnation. "Joseph," I introduced them, "this is Mercy." Which is what I'd been calling her up to now, not being sure about how to address a nun. Would a uniform "Sister" do, or was that too formal? Maybe it wasn't formal enough.

"My dear," is how Iris Rocke got around the problem, after dabbing at a tear and kissing her great-granddaughter on both cheeks. "My dear, it is so wonderful to meet you!" A minute later she was addressing me similarly. I'd enquired why a uniformed bobby was crunching a desultory path up and down Iris's gravel and she'd replied that Inspector Vann had thought it a good idea. "Because of recent events, my dear." We were then led up the wide central stairway and allocated bedrooms with tasseled curtains and orchids in cut-glass vases. Mercy disappeared in the direction of a bathroom and I posed the question again.

"Mrs. Rocke." I resisted shaking her. "What is going on?"

She picked a tiny feather off her sleeve. "Louise was here this afternoon."

So much for martinis in the tropics. My right eye twitched. "What did she say? Where's she been?"

"I don't know where she's been, but she came here to ask me for money. She said that Bryton's murder wasn't anything to do with the casino but was a warning to her. A man she'd been doing business with had had Bryton killed and she needed money in order to get out of the country. I told her I wouldn't help and she left. I then rang the police. I don't think —" Iris's mouth twisted into a smile, "that we need tell Mercy this tonight, do you?"

"Oh no," I agreed, "there's no need to tell her all the news at once."

Joseph did the cooking. I had no idea whether in his capacity as secretary he could actually type, but he could certainly whip up a mean soufflé. The dining room had a long central table, a chandelier, and walls decorated with portraits and landscapes from the last century. It filled me with a definite sense of déja vu. All we needed now was a body under one of the chairs.

"They are beautiful, aren't they?" Iris saw me

studying the centerpiece of tiger lilies, floating in a wide bowl.

"Very," I said. They were, but I was finding it difficult to concentrate on the aesthetics of the evening.

"They were Bryton's favorite." Mercy had said how sorry she was about Bryton's death but throughout dinner the conversation had centered on Mercy herself, rather than on her family. She told us about her work in Nicaragua, which had largely consisted of criss-crossing the countryside in a Jeep, immunizing children in remote villages, and about her work in Romania now. She described not only the orphanage but also her travels through the Carpathian mountains and the Transylvanian Alps. The winters were bitter, the summers baking. The Danube, flowing from the Black Forest into the Black Sea, carried with it the history of Europe, the growth and disintegration of empires. Since the completion of a system of canals in the mid 1980s it was possible to travel over three thousand kilometers from Germany to the Black Sea, via Vienna, Budapest and Belgrade . . .

I half-listened to this while studying the faces of my dinner companions. Mercy, Iris and Joseph: the nun flanked by the con artist and the hit man. Somebody should paint a triptych. From over Mercy's head a ruddy-faced woman in a bonnet winked down, a liver spaniel at her feet. Life, the woman seemed to be saying, is what we make it. The spaniel's feet were muddy on its mistress's carpet, its eyes amused. My life would be spent with April. We would have a wide table, scrubbed with salt. I would buy a Balinese dragon in red and gold and hang it from the kitchen ceiling. A summer palace.

"More wine, Miss Cross?" Joseph's offer came during a lull in the conversation.

"Yes," I said. "Please." I was drinking more than usual, but why not? There was nothing for me to do here but observe. As the wine filled my glass I looked at the two women opposite me and wondered what they really made of each other. One had a life that could be laid out in company and read like a book: here is where I bought a straw hat and sailed down a river; there is where I was stranded halfway up a dirt road with a broken axle. The other's life was only hinted at; a shape hidden under layers of fabric; a man's body crumpled at the bottom of the stairs. Looking up I saw Mercy frown slightly, shift her napkin on her lap. No, I was wrong. I was oversimplifying her, as I'd oversimplified Perry.

"Miss Cross." All of a sudden Iris and the others were standing, napkins in one hand, glasses in the other. "For pudding there is cake and I think we might move to my study for that."

In the study were velvet armchairs, a desk with embossed leather, and a Victorian screen decorated with hand-tinted flowers frozen under layers of varnish. Ignoring the chairs, Mercy sat herself down on the carpet, in front of the open fire. "My mother," she said. "Louise. Have you told her about me?"

"No." Iris's hands disappeared into the deep pockets of her long cardigan. "No, I haven't told her yet. I was hoping we might get to know each other a little first. I realize this must seem very strange."

The shrug that accompanied this suggested that

the niceties of the rest of the world had little to do with her. As if in agreement her great-granddaughter sat on the floor eating chocolate cake. I thought the whole show was pretty weird myself, although I managed to hide the fact. That is, until I saw the brass door handle apparently turning by itself.

The handle turned, the door silently opened, and as a figure stepped into the room I jumped to my feet, dropping my plate and silver fork in the process.

"Sit down." Louise sounded irritated. I sat.

"That goes for everyone," she added. In her right hand was a gun, and on the gun was a silencer. She pointed the combination at Joseph, but addressed Iris. "You see, Mummy, I didn't leave today, after all. Instead I've been sitting in my old room upstairs, doing a lot of thinking. And for the past five minutes I've been listening outside the door. Bad manners, I know, but how else am I supposed to find out what's going on in this family? Little Miss Muffet here, for instance, now no one thought to tell me that she'd been found. I wonder why that was?"

"You're Louise." Mercy didn't sound frightened, merely curious. I was so scared I felt I was going to throw up, or wet myself, or both.

"Yes." Louise nodded. "Ironic, isn't it? Mummy here always wanted a nun for a daughter, but somehow she got it wrong. It took a couple of faggots to get it right."

It was my turn next. "If only you'd confided in me, Tor. You see, I thought Bry had employed you in order to check up on my business dealings, and when I told my partners that they got very annoyed indeed. So annoyed that they killed my poor, dear sister. Isn't it amazing, the problems caused by lack of trust?"

Taking a step back she gestured at Iris. "You're going to open the safe. After the safe is open I'm going to lock you all into the pantry. I leave with the money, and no one gets hurt."

Her hair caught the firelight and her face was relaxed and confident. Too relaxed, too confident, to be entirely sane. She nodded at Iris, who carefully stood up and walked past the screen to a picture hanging opposite the door. The picture swung out to reveal a brown safe. The combination took a matter of seconds.

"Stand in the middle of the room."

Iris did as she was told and Louise walked over to the safe door and pulled it open. She pulled out a wad of banknotes, which she then shoved into one of her coat pockets. "Thank you. I'll try not to spend it all at once."

I glanced across at Joseph but his face was impassive, his hands resting on his knees.

"Now," Louise said, "in a couple of minutes we're all taking a walk out back to the kitchen. I'm going to turn the hall lights off, just in case our policeman friend looks in through a front window. If he does I strongly recommend that you don't make a sound. Mummy will lead the way, followed by Tor." She looked at Joseph. "You come next. My darling daughter will be in front of me, and if anything happens I will shoot her. Is that clear?"

What was clear to me was that I'd always known this was how it was going to happen, herded along a dark hallway.

"Right." Louise stood back against the wall. "You can stand up now."

I couldn't breathe, I couldn't do it.

The gun swung in my direction. "That includes you, Tor."

I stood.

At the end of the hall Iris pushed a door open and I stumbled after her into a large kitchen. I was aware of wooden shelves and cupboards and a strong smell that I couldn't place. There was a central table, which Louise kept between us and her.

"Well done," she said. "On the table are four lengths of cord and four scarves. Joseph, you're going to tie everyone's hands behind their backs, then you'll gag them. I'll tie you up at the end. You can start with her." She pointed at Mercy.

Mercy put her head on one side. "May God forgive you." She said it as if it was something she'd been thinking about for a very long time, and as if it was a response to more than being locked in a cupboard, or even abandoned at birth. She took a step forward. "Louise," she said, "God's grace is infinite."

Louise's smile was ironic and as I stared at her face I thought, how? How was she going to tie Joseph up while holding the gun? And then I realized that's what Mercy was talking about, about the fact that Louise intended to kill us. Joseph — I glanced across to him — why the fuck didn't he do something? All he did, however, was move to the edge of the table and pick up a piece of blue cord.

My legs felt as if they were about to crumple; once we were tied up Louise would simply shoot Joseph and then pick the rest of us off one by one.

Time, we needed more time. "You murdered your husband." My voice came out as a croak. Do something, somebody. Anything.

"Yes." Louise's response was matter-of-fact. "You're quite right, Tor."

"And your father."

She was looking at me. If I kept her looking at me it might give Joseph a chance. He could leap the table with a knife, use a piece of cord as a garrotte.

"You murdered your father, too."

"I did."

Next to me, Iris's hands were deep in her pockets and she pulled them close into her body, as if she were hugging herself. "Do you —" Her voice was urgent, "repent?"

Louise's head tipped slightly back. "Oh yes." Her laugh was quite merry. "Yes, I —"

The bullet caught her square in the chest. Her arms, and then her body, lifted in a graceful motion, as if she were dancing. Yes, I thought as I watched her, that's what it is: I'd recognized the smell that had bothered me when we came into the room.

It was the smell of white spirit.

Epilogue

"Highly inflammatory," April muttered.

I studied the ceiling rose. "You mean inflammable. It most certainly is, it was only then I realized what a dastardly deed she'd been planning."

"I'm not talking about the white spirit, Victoria. I've been brooding about what you said earlier this evening, how you'd been worried I was embarrassed by your job."

"Oh." I rolled over on the pillow and looked at her. We'd just made love for what would be the last time in April's Battersea bedroom. For the last time on April's futon too, if it came to that: we'd taken Mr. Rabin up on his offer of a beautiful oak bed, full of happy memories. "Well, it would be understandable if you were embarrassed. Lawyers are definitely white-collar, while private investigators . . ." My right hand slid up her firm belly and across to her wrist. "I guess I count as a bit of rough, eh?"

Flipping over, she surprised me by pinning both my wrists above my head. "I'm going to get that scarf."

"April Tate, we've got a table booked for dinner at Gino's." I gave a mock-resisting wriggle.

"I'm going to get that scarf, lady, and I'm going to show you exactly what I can do with it."

Which is exactly what she did.

April and Alicia, the two most important women in my life. Excepting Ma, of course. I watched as Alicia's fingers tugged at the strap of the watch I'd given her five years ago, for her thirtieth birthday. "Sweet Jesus," she was saying. "I will never, I mean never, go away again. Didn't you try to stop her, April?"

As April reached for the carafe a pair of blue eyes met mine. "Oh, I think Victoria looks after herself pretty well."

"Looks after herself! If the old lady hadn't happened to be packing a pistol in her pocket they would all have been shot. What's going to happen about that, anyway?"

I raised an eyebrow in April's direction. "Iris isn't in too much legal hot water, is she? Shooting Louise was self-defense, there's no question about that, and I can't imagine that at her age they'll give her a seriously hard time about toting an unlicensed gun. It wasn't Iris's anyway, it was Joseph's. When the police arrived she explained that she and Joseph had been concerned in case Louise did turn up sometime, and they'd decided Iris should carry the gun because they knew Louise would watch Joseph very carefully."

"Victoria." Paola had materialized at my left shoulder. "I am sorry but tonight there are no sardines."

"No sardines?" There were always sardines.

She shrugged. "I take your order through to the kitchen and Gino says to tell you he has no sardines. He suggests the *tagliatelle con spinaci*."

Resistance was pointless. "Tell Gino I'm in his hands."

"Do you think that's what would have happened?" Diane looked at me thoughtfully.

"What's that?"

"That you would have been shot?"

"I don't know, I don't know whether Louise planned to lock us in the pantry, and then set fire to the house; or if she was going to shoot us all first. She'd already got away with two murders that looked like accidents, so I suspect she was hoping she could pull it off again."

Steph shuddered. "Can you believe it?" She poured herself another mineral water, then offered the bottle to Alicia.

"Thanks." Alicia filled her glass. Steph was driving herself home but Alicia hadn't brought her car with her tonight. I smiled across the table: third time lucky, I hoped. Alicia smiled back.

"The bit that I really cannot believe," Anchee said, "is this Western superstition about saving your immortal soul at the last minute. It's not as though she meant it, is it?"

A priest had arrived to administer the last rites and Iris Rocke had calmly informed him that her granddaughter had said she repented. Her greatest con ever.

Diane cleared a space as Paola reappeared with a basket of garlic bread. "And Mercy will one day inherit all the loot?"

"She will. No doubt she'll turn the house into an orphanage. There'll be children sliding down every banister."

April's knee nudged mine. "We're moving house tomorrow."

"Yes," I said, "south of the river." Which suited me just fine.

Also of interest:

Penny Sumner
The End of April
A Victoria Cross Mystery

Victoria Cross, archivist and professional PI, returns from New York at her Oxford professor aunt's request to transcribe Victorian pornography...

Then she meets the gorgeous April Tate: law student, lesbian activist and anti-pornography campaigner. But April is in grave danger and, when death intrudes, suddenly and violently, Victoria Cross realises it could soon be the end of April...

'Deftly written and cleverly crafted...We will hear more of Victoria Cross.' *Gay Scotland*

Crime Fiction £5.99
ISBN 0 7043 4358 4

Jen Green, editor
Reader, I Murdered Him

With original stories from Sara Paretsky, Penny Sumner, Barbara
Wilson, Amanda Cross and many more, *Reader, I Murdered Him*
showcases sixteen suspenseful murder mysteries by some of the
best women crime writers in the world today.

A classic of the genre and runaway bestseller, this exciting
collection offers razor-sharp solutions to the problems of the
outgrown husband, the office bozo and the holiday bore...

'Entertaining and witty.' *Living*

'Splendid yarns.' *Ms London*

Crime Fiction £5.99
ISBN 0 7043 4159 X

Helen Windrath, editor
Reader, I Murdered Him, Too

'A woman's gotta do what a woman's gotta do: holding eye contact, I smile right back...'

Crimes in convents, murder in stately homes and bodies lost at sea. Hot on the trail are hard-drinking investigators, academic sleuths and determined amateurs. The best in the business are back again.

Following the runaway success of *Reader, I Murdered Him* – now an acclaimed classic of the genre – *Reader, I Murdered Him, Too* sees the razor-sharp return of Penny Sumner, Sara Paretsky, Val McDermid, Meg O'Brien and many more, with a lethal combination of classic crime stories.

Crime Fiction £5.99
ISBN 0 7043 4363 0

Mary Wings
She Came by the Book
The Third Emma Victor Mystery

'Roll over Raymond Chandler, and tell Philip Marlowe the news: the lady has a pistol in her pocket.' *Elle*

It's been twenty years since Emma Victor's boss, the flamboyant politician Howard Blooming, was assassinated. Now she's promised to deliver his private papers and their secrets into safekeeping. The opening of the Howard Blooming Memorial Archive seems to provide Victor with a golden opportunity. But her mission is soon placed in deadly jeopardy when the chief archivist suddenly succumbs to cyanide poisoning...

'She writes with a brisk charm.' Colin Dexter, creator of Inspector Morse

'Mary Wings has continued the Chandler tradition in her own brilliant style.' *Dominion*

'Well-paced and a terrible tease.' *Pink Paper*

Crime Fiction £5.99
ISBN 0 7043 4432 7